Critical Acclaim for DEAR VENUS

'Very sexy, very funny and at times very sad, this marvellously intelligent novel (about adultery in the suburbs) provides needlesharp insight into what men and women feel about really want from each other. In the tradition of *Les Liaisons Dangereuses*, DEAR VENUS is a comedy of lack of manners. It made me want to behave deliciously badly and be a much better person all at the same time. I look forward to Cassandra Brooke's next novel very much' – Jilly Cooper

'Anyone who loves fly-on-the-wall documentaries and overhearing conversations in pubs will love Cassandra Brooke's quirky new novel' – *Yorkshire Evening Post*

'An enjoyable romp' – *Today*

About the Author

Since she graduated in English Literature from Oxford University, Cassandra Brooke has lived a restless and festive life – as an art historian, journalist and critic, lecturer and travel guide, broadcaster, scriptwriter for television and radio, historical novelist, Arts Council committee dragon, and as a campaigner for such worthy causes as the preservation of tropical rain forests, the protection of endangered vultures, and women's membership of Lord's cricket ground. Between these activities Cassandra has lived in France, achieved two marriages, three children and a large house in south-west London. She has written a sequel to *Dear Venus*, called *With Much Love*.

CASSANDRA BROOKE

Dear Venus

POCKET
BOOKS

New York London Toronto Sydney Tokyo Singapore

First published in Great Britain by Pocket Books, 1993
An imprint of Simon & Schuster Ltd
A Paramount Communications Company

Reprinted 1993

Simon & Schuster Ltd
West Garden Place
Kendal Street
London W1 2AQ

Simon & Schuster of Australia Pty Ltd
Sydney

A CIP catalogue record for this book is
available from the British Library

ISBN 0–671–71552–6

Typeset by The Electronic Book Factory Ltd,
Fife, Scotland
Printed and bound by
Harper*Collins* Manufacturing,
Glasgow

For Jason

September

Dear Janice,

A scrawl from among the packing cases.

Here we are, unhijacked. Until we get our flat, this splendid address will reach me. No street name on the letterhead, please note – I suspect no Brit on the embassy staff ever troubled to learn the Greek alphabet well enough to decipher the street sign.

What a dreadful city this is; I'd forgotten. For God's sake write before I die of lead-poisoning and fetta cheese. And of course I want to hear about your own move upmarket to London W4 – Chiswick or Hammersmith, is it – something like that? (Better Greek restaurants there than here, I bet.) And you must tell me, is it really a fresh start for you and Harry, as you put it? I have my . . . no, I'll shut up. Anyway, you know what I think of Harry. At least the kid's away at school now, so you only have yourselves to fight for, or fight *against*.

The ambassador's a berk. Piers brought him a

3

Stilton from Paxton and Whitfield, and from his smile you'd think he'd just vomited it. Oh Janice, I have to be a First Secretary's wife – a gracious adornment. How does one do it? Three years in this Hellenic backwater, where you can't drink the water and the wine is worse.

What is a Jewish slag doing here?

Lots of love. And write! Brighten my expatriate hours.

Ruth.

1 River Mews
London W4

September 28th

Dearest Ruth,

Wonderful to hear that you've arrived along with the ambassadorial Stilton.

We've made it, too. River Mews – how do you like that? There's no river within sight, I have to say, and the only thing that mews is the cats. Everyone in the street has them, including one undoctored Tom who is the source of powerful friction among the neighbours. Talk in our alley is of nothing but electronic cat-flaps. That shows you we've indeed moved upmarket.

Let me paint the scene for you. The street's actually tiny. Ten houses, that's all, and on one side only. On the other side is a wall and then a churchyard where someone I've never heard of is buried. Next to it are two tennis courts which I'm longing to use in the summer. Nine of the houses are semi-detached – elegant, early Victorian, white, polished-looking, two floors and a basement. Ours at No 1 is the only single house, and that's merely because a road-widening scheme twenty years ago sliced off the other half. So a dual carriageway rattles by beyond a hedge of tall cypresses, thank God. At the other end of the street (sorry, mews!) is a path leading to an old reservoir, now a nature reserve. All day we have the back view of twitchers in woolly hats and binocs, and no doubt in the summer it'll be a breeding ground for some rare and protected form of mosquito.

In other words, my dear, it's a *cul-de-sac*, which sets me wondering (worrying?) what *cul* Harry may soon lay in the sack; though after our 'trial separation' he promises to be good. 'It's been a nightmare,' he says. There were tears in his eyes. Oh Ruth, don't tell me I'm an idiot just yet; I'm so longing for it to be right. I hated being alone, that washed-up feeling. And Harry knows me, there's such comfort in that. I can be awful and he just puts his arms round me, and I melt. Everything's forgotten. I think I love him – that perverse stubborn feeling which won't go even after all the years I've told it to. We even make love again, sort of. I suppose I feel grateful that at least it's me and not some bimbo – I can hear how that exasperates you – but then you've got it all, lovers as well.

Shit, I didn't mean to whinge at you. Let me tell you about the neighbours – we of River Mews (I shall have to get used to that). Well, one of them threw a welcome party for us. He's an architect, Bill something-or-other. Well-known, I believe. A beanpole of a man with precious hands – you know what I mean. The house is full of ingenious gadgetry, like a laboratory for living. Everything doubles up as something else; the beds are store-cupboards or filing systems, the coffee-table's a CD player. Nothing as crude as a light-switch; you just breathe on the wall. The loo flushes when you get up (what do men do?). And of course solar panels everywhere that make the place look like a carnation farm from the outside. The wife's plain with gigantic tits; perhaps they double up as something else, too. Harry kept gazing at them in wonder. Nina, she's called. I rather liked her, but she introduced me like a stray she'd found, 'This is our new No 1.' And all the others did the same: 'I'm No 3,' 'I'm No 8,' and so on, as if they hadn't got names. I tried not to giggle. I was wearing my Jean Muir dress – second-hand of course, from you-know-where. Very clingy, I'd almost forgotten I had a figure. No 10 spotted it, and from her look will have told everyone we're stinking rich by now. Harry got some kudos for being recognised – you know, 'This is Harry Blakemore, ITN, Warsaw' – but the woman (No 5, I think) then spoilt it by asking if he enjoyed doing the weather forecast. She *was* very pissed.

The strange thing about moving here is the feeling of being assessed. I asked Harry what he felt, and he just shrugged and said he felt they were all rather boring. 'Bourgeois,' he added. Christ, what does he think we are? Besides, I could see him sizing up the local talent. Spotted him enjoying an intimate little number (No 2 –

sorry!) with a movie director's wife (or perhaps not) who kept shaking her hair at him. I cursed him for being so good-looking. 'Don't be ridiculous,' he said afterwards, 'the woman's a moron.' Huh! That never stopped him before. She was blonde.

Actually they're not boring, at least not all of them. I think people show a corporate face; perhaps it comes of sharing small interests. You have to find the larger ones they don't share. They're fairly motley. Two doctors (husband and wife, not in partnership). A builder (ghastly with a voice like the *Spitting Image* Ted Heath). An ad-man (ultra-smooth). The movie director (with an eye that roves to your breasts). A Labour candidate – would be – called Courtenay Gascoigne (hardly a name to wow them in Tower Hamlets, I'd have thought), and a breeder of a wife with hands shaped for changing nappies. She's said to write long, significant novels. Christ, aren't I a bitch! Then, who else? Oh yes, a shy historian who fancied me, and some sort of RA portrait painter who didn't. And a silent TV producer Harry knows slightly – does things on ecology – oil-slicks, acid rain and such.

Some of them asked what I did, and I said, 'Antique dealer,' which is sort of true, isn't it? I wasn't going to let on it was a junk stall once a month in the Acton Leisure Centre. Nor was I going to say I painted, or they would have tried to look interested and asked, 'What?' Can you imagine my saying, 'Murals,' when I've only done two, one for Clive's bedroom and the other for my mother's loo? Perhaps I should have said,

7

'Encaustic – like Leonardo da Vinci,' hoping they didn't know what a cock-up Leonardo made of it.

Oh Ruth, do I make it sound jolly? Or dire? I suppose it was both. I felt a fake. Fake happy. Smiling by numbers, pretending I belonged to their safe, achieving world. But then I remembered what it was like being alone. Separated. I looked up 'separate' in the dictionary not long ago, and it said, 'Divide, sunder.' That's just what I felt – sundered. Harry's all kinds of a shit, but it was intolerable without him. Can you imagine what I missed most all those months? Not sex. Not having so little money. It was not having him mix my evening drink – putting ice and a slice of lime in the vodka and tonic. It was him laughing at how I always drape my knickers over the towel-rail. It was even him keeping me awake snoring. Daft, isn't it? God, I hope it will work out this time; I don't think I can stand it if it doesn't.

Hey, I met an acupuncturist who told me (it was a *she*) you can put some zip into your libido by pressing a spot just below your knee. *You* won't need it, but I'm in there, pressing.

Write again soon, diplomat's lady. I miss our long chats and your scurrilous stories.

Love – and to lovely Piers.

Janice.

Dear Piers,

I enjoyed your elegant speech at the college reunion (I so admire the ease with which diplomats lie). But wasn't it a diabolical occasion? Old alumni never die, they merely bore each other to death.

There was no chance to give you this address before you took off for Athens – though maybe Janice has given it to Ruth by now. You asked me what I felt about it all, and looked surprised. As well you might. To be truthful, I don't quite know how it came about either. I was rather getting used to bachelorhood, and being away so much for ITN I hardly felt the loneliness of it. Not that there was much of that; a fair passage of birds in the night, unfamiliar faces on dawn pillows, silent breakfasts ('Do you take tea or coffee?'). None the less here we are again, to my surprise. And – strangely – pleasure.

What happened was a dinner together in Chelsea. I was just back from Eastern Europe. There was a message from Janice on the answerphone about Clive's new school – please could I possibly ring? So I did. Suggested dinner. I hadn't seen her for six months and was expecting frostbite. Not at all. It was very relaxed and easy. She was looking extremely sexy in a low-cut number. Jesus, I thought, I fancy her. Then she invited me back to her place. No messing about. All bright-eyed. Lots of leg and perfume. And that was it.

The odd thing was how natural it seemed. Something to do with it being so familiar. No awkwardnesses – legs in the wrong place, cut lips. One-night-stands aren't exactly ballet, are they? Anyway, in the morning I didn't know what to say. 'Thank you sweetheart, and goodbye,' didn't seem right, though I half-hoped she might say that. She didn't. It was soft looks and, 'Darling, why don't we . . . ? So much to throw away. The kid.' Gentlest blackmail. Do you think I should have said no? I couldn't, and actually I didn't want to. I wanted to be near her. I wanted to re-open that chapter in my life because I suddenly realised how much I'd missed it. Life felt complete again.

So we bought the house in record time – a fat mortgage, of course. And here we are, No 1, River Mews. Now you know.

By the way, I'm off to darkest Poland again in about a month's time. The same old Lech Walesa trail. But if Papandreou snuffs it, or goes on trial (surely not), I may get sent to your neck of the woods. Are First Secretaries allowed to get pissed with itinerant journalists, I wonder?

See you some time, old mate, and I'll keep in touch.

All the best,

Harry.

October

October 2nd

Dearest Ruth,

I'm bursting to tell you the news. I have a *commission*! A real commission, for a mural. The architect I told you about – the bean-pole with the bosomy wife – well, I plucked up courage and told him what I did (as though I'd done hundreds, everything but the Sistine Chapel) and he asked to see some drawings. So I rushed home and did some quickly – tried to make them look old and soiled. And fuck me, he commissioned one. A river scene; quite clever, I have to admit. Makes his study look like a houseboat, with his dog about to jump into the water. He laughed. And he really liked it.

Isn't it wonderful! I'm a professional. Wow!

Harry's being absolutely sweet.

Can't wait to start. My life, too.

In haste – masses of love,

Janice.

October 15th

Dear Janice,

Your letters – the long and the short – were waiting in the First Secretary's pigeon-hole when I got back yesterday. Great to hear from you – and of course about your commission. Trif. Congrats and stuff. Yes, I've been away (wait for it, details to follow). I really had to. No proper place to live yet. Piers up to his eyes in paper-work (he howls like King Lear). So I took off for the Peloponnese in the little VW we've bought. Ruth on the loose (or, you may think, cunt on the hunt). Greece miraculous in the autumn. Very hot still, but sharp and clear, no longer shimmering, and not seething with tourists either. I'd never been to Olympia, or to Mistra – and what a place (though I have reasons for so-thinking; be patient, my good Protestant girl).

First – you. Your second letter capped the one before it in a way. I haven't known you so bubbly for years. Just that one line, 'Harry's being absolutely sweet.' I'm glad. Perhaps he's learnt something. Or perhaps you have. But the sweet-and-sour first letter; it wouldn't be true to say that I know how you feel being back with Harry, because I don't. I've never tried to repair anything – what's torn is torn. (Piers is a special case; he never tears.) But I *can* imagine. You're a timid person; at least you believe you are. I know I've said it often, but you did settle for the louche Harry frightfully young. Were you a virgin? I can't remember. No, there was that law student with acne, wasn't there, but that couldn't have been exactly life-enhancing. You said he had a willy like a sardine. So you've never had any bigger fish, except Harry, and how big is he? Not as big as his ego, I bet.

What I'm saying – as a dedicated wandering spirit – is you really don't know enough about men. You expect them to be what they're not – loyal and faithful and loving. But Janice, only the wimps are that, the ones who long to be mothered. Attractive men are hunter-gatherers; they've merely substituted careers and crumpet for bears and bison. And why not? If women don't want to be doormats they should stop breeding and cooking back in the cave and go out and join the hunt. I suppose you'll say that's fine for me because I don't care a damn about children. But children bring themselves up if you give them a chance, don't they? Most mothers don't let them because they're too scared to be anything other than mothers, and ruin their children as a result. I'm fed up with women bleating from the cave.

Oh God, why do I always end up lecturing you? It's a very ugly side of me, and I'm not sure how much of all that I believe, anyway. A reaction against generations of Yiddish mamas.

Now I'll tell you about my travels. Olympia was magical. The perfect ruins should be romantic – a spurious sense of wandering in the past when we have absolutely no idea what it would really have been like, and wouldn't like it if we did. All those columns of the Temple of Zeus lying there like sliced Blackpool Rock:

you expect to see the lettering all through, 'Olympic Games BC 400'. They look so beautiful in desolation. An American next to me said, 'Why don't they put them back up?' 'Because it'd look like a railway station,' I said. 'They could do with one of those here,' he added. His wife looked quite shocked. In the old stadium close by, German fraus in Lacoste T-shirts were pounding out the two hundred metres with tits akimbo. 'The Spartans used to do it naked,' I said to my American. 'I'm glad this lot don't – they'd tip over,' he replied, at which point his wife tugged him off to lunch. I'm not a woman wives like.

The magic came in the evening. I bribed one of the guards to let me stay after dark. And then the moon came up, full moon, over the trees. The whole place was silver and black. I sat and listened to the owls and a million frogs. Such peace. Why do ruined places do that to you? Is it that they spin you out of time?

Then across the central Peloponnese to Mistra. It's like Pompeii on a steep hillside, except that the old road zig-zags down from ancient church to ancient church. Apparently it used to be the capital of the Byzantine Empire. So, wonderful frescoes everywhere. And nobody around but me. Well, not entirely true. There was this Greek guide. Not much more than a kid, but terribly pretty. A shock of curly black hair and eyes like Picasso. I tell you, Janice, I am not a nice person to know. What were my first thoughts, do you suppose? Not, 'Do I fancy this guy?' Not, 'Do I want a toyboy for the afternoon?' Not even, 'Where on earth do I take him?' You know the very first thing that came into my mind, even before I realised I wanted him, was, 'Did I bring a condom with me?'

Well, I had, though the young satyr didn't know what it was and kept detumescing each time I tried to put it on. I may have given him a castration complex for life. When I did finally succeed he didn't know where to put it, and I began to feel like a cow being prodded by the farmer's stick. It was obviously a 'first' for him, and the experience was so traumatic I imagined it might be a 'last', too. Admittedly the environment couldn't have helped his peace of mind: it *was* a church. I'd never fucked in a church before. I kept saying to myself, 'This is not desecration, I'm Jewish.' It was a derelict church, though; do you think that makes it any better? In the end he managed it with a long sob like a dying warrior; and just as well because at that moment I heard distant voices approaching, heavily Germanic, and we had to dress at speed and pretend to be admiring the frescoes.

I suppose you'll want to know if I enjoyed it. Not a lot, I have to say: no heavenly music, no comets racing across my eyeballs. The pleasures of youthful corruption are mostly in the mind, I realise. I kept thinking, 'Piers would do this so much better,' which irritated me. That's not what one is supposed to feel in moments of infidelity, is it?

Afterwards he was sweet and took my hand while he showed me round all the other churches. I wasn't sure if this was gratitude or whether he hoped for a repeat performance in all of them. Then came the problem of how the hell to get rid of him. This wasn't easy without being unkind. But hunter-gatherer had become lap-dog. I pleaded the conventional headache, and next morning had to leave the hotel at dawn to avoid the Romeo bit. As I drove back towards Athens I kept thinking, 'This is absurd, I'm thirty-five.'

From your bad friend, with love and bruises,

Ruth.

1 River Mews
London W4

October 22nd

Dearest Ruth,

Oh, I'm having such fun. Didn't know I could be so happy. All the storm-clouds blown away. I've been longing to tell you about the house (I seem to have told you about everything else *but* the house). Well, first of all I love it. The architect at No 7 (my patron!) tells me rather heavily that it's early Victorian but still keeping Georgian proportions (more than can be said of his wife, whose proportions are those of an oil rig). Anyway, that means tall windows, wide panes, handsome portico, narrow hallway, but off it the front and back rooms have been knocked into one to make a huge living-room that catches the sun at both ends (not at once). Upstairs are three bedrooms – one tiny – and a bathroom *en suite* with the master bedroom (which makes me a mistress, doesn't it? You always said I should be). So even when Clive's home for the holidays there's a spare room whenever you want to flee shitty Athens. Then in the semi-basement is what's become Harry's study, another small bathroom next to it, and the kitchen-dining-room leading out into the back-garden which is quite big, forty feet – I measured it but haven't got round to thinking about the garden yet. Oh, there's an attic too, reached by a perilous ladder and a trap-door you have to push up with your head. I got a splinter in my scalp the first time I used it.

The only thing is – wait for it – the decor. Scunthorpe Bordello, Harry calls it. Yuk-coloured paint combed to look like wood – actually it's combed to look like yuk. But the *pièce de resistance* is the ceiling, *all* the ceilings. These have beautiful plaster mouldings round the edges and a rosette thing in the centre; and can you believe it, they're *pink*! Boiled-sweet pink, Diana Dors lipstick. No cadillac was ever pinker. So, between the combed yuk and the knickerdropper glory we hold tasteful conversations and listen to Mozart. Marital bliss. Needless to say, when we have some money we'll have a blitzkrieg, but for the time being it's Yuk Villas.

What else? Oh yes. Because of the mural I'm getting to know some of the wives. They pop in and have a look (probably to have another look at me). Nina – she's the architect's wife – seems to be the hub of social life here: pillar of the local conservation society, anti-aircraft noise, etc. Very sweet. Also mad on tennis like me, which is great. We shared a bottle of wine yesterday and she told me she used to be at the *Folies-Bergère*. From her tits I can understand why.

Nina's been giving me the low-down on the others

(refer to my earlier letter for cast list). Apparently the historian's wife is an alcoholic who screws anyone who comes to the door. I'll have to watch her. The portrait painter's wife on the other hand belongs to some weird religious sect that doesn't believe in sex at all, though Nina says if I saw her (which I since have) I'd think how relieved the husband must be. She actually called in today and pressed some literature on me, printed on rice-paper, then gazed at the mural and said how spiritual water was. She looks like a spider-monkey in drag.

I also had a visit from the woman at No 10, wife of the TV director, the one who was envious of my Jean Muir dress. I was in jeans this time and she was dressed all ethnic as though she'd raided every folk museum from Fiji to Marrakesh. What a bitch I am. But she was so bloody patronising. Amanda, she's called – pronounces it as though she's got weights in her throat. Ah-man-dah. A musician (or sort of once, I suspect) with terribly clever children, she told me. I hate people with clever children. Do you know what? She looked at the mural for a minute and then said, 'Darling, you've got such pretty hair.' The cow! I could have kicked her. Then she said something about Harry being so good at his job and wasn't I proud of him? 'What about my mural?', I wanted to say, 'I'm proud of that, too.'

In fact, she's the only tricky one. Everyone else is lovely – Harry too – he brings me flowers, we make love from time to time. I just wish he wouldn't call me 'dear'. I bet your Greek toyboy didn't call you that. I loved that story of yours. In a church! Where did you do it? On the altar? Disgraceful you are, a First Secretary's wife, too.

But tell me seriously – I've never asked you before – do you tell Piers about your escapades? I know you have an 'open marriage', but how open can a marriage be without falling apart? Does he care? Doesn't he feel jealous? And what do you feel when he has affairs? Maybe it's immature of me or something, but what does love mean if you can make love to other people as well? I know I couldn't bear it. It's what broke Harry and me apart. Loving for me is giving and giving everything; there's no room for share-outs.

How I change moods, don't I? A minute ago I was telling you how much I loved hearing about your romp in the church, and here I am preaching fidelity. I suppose you'll tell me it's because I'm a vicarious slut who's only slept with two men in her life and one of those was a sardine.

Maybe, maybe. What I do know is that Harry's what I want, and I am really happy. I'll leave playing the field to you, just so long as you tell me about it. Is that a bargain?

Lots of love,

Janice.

October 24th

Dear Piers,

No, I didn't expect you to put belladonna in Papandreou's ouzo in order to get me an assignment. Anyway, he has his own bella donna: voluptuous baggage, isn't she? Have you met her? I like it – Prime Minister's perks – splendidly old-fashioned and brazen, like a Borgia pope.

It's Bucharest in a short while, not Poland, so I'm informed by the powers-that-be. For how long I don't know. *Ceausescu est mort: vive Ceausescu.* We live in exciting times, not that you'd know it in River Mews. The hottest news here is Janice's mural. Seems to keep her busy.

All the best,

Harry.

October 29th,

Darling,

So you really are enjoying the new school. That's wonderful. You know, I was terribly worried at first because I never liked the idea of boarding-school. But you seemed so determined, and since you're now eleven, Daddy and I thought you probably knew best.

Shall I tell you about the new house? You only saw it that one afternoon before we moved in. Your room's all ready now for when you come home, and I've put your Pooh Bear posters up on the wall, as well as your Tottenham Hotspur photos.

Well, it's really lovely here. And lovely too that Daddy will be here with us now that he's no longer spending so much time working abroad. I hated being without him all that time. The great thing about the house is having all this space to rattle around in. I'm afraid the pink decoration you liked so much is probably going to have to go. Daddy says it gives him a headache. But you can keep it in your room if you want to, though it's not Tottenham Hotspur colours, is it?

The people are nice here. There's a boy about your age at the end of the street – No 10. His mother's a musician. She came to watch me doing the painting I told you about the other afternoon, and seemed pleasant. A bit oddly dressed. Then there's a very sweet woman at

No 7 who used to be a dancer, though she's got rather large since then. I can't imagine her in a tutu. Next door to them is a man who wants to be a Labour MP but seems to spend most of his time getting his wife pregnant. And next door to *us* is a successful (so I gather) movie director (he recently made something called *Pools of Love* which I haven't seen) who has lots of secretaries I keep confusing with his wife because they all look rather alike. They have loud parties and seem to break a lot of glasses.

So it's all lively stuff and I hope you'll enjoy living here.

You must tell me whether you got into the school football team, and I hope the parcel of goodies reached you OK.

Lots and lots of love, and from Daddy of course,

Mummy.

1 River Mews
London W4

October 30th

Dearest Ruth,

Glorious autumn weather, and let me tell you I've now discovered the garden. We never had one before – only that gloomy back yard you'll remember which the estate agents described as a patio.

Here we have space. Not enough for a tennis court, alas, but real space none the less. Shrubs – God knows what they are, but Spindle our new kitten absails from them – and flowers – autumn crocuses, I believe they are, sort of purply things in clusters. Nina says the previous owners loved bulbs and I should wait till spring before planting anything new. But I long to make it my own, like the house. I want to put in things that sound nice, like heart's-ease, corncockle, rosemary and rue. Maybe they look like weeds, I wouldn't know, but I want a garden full of lovely names I can recite, and then pick them like Perdita in *The Winter's Tale* and spread them out for my Florizel – do you remember that wonderful line, 'Like a bank for love to lie and play on'?

I'm being silly and girlish, aren't I, but that's how I feel. Harry's my Florizel, all anew and cuddly, and I love him. How did it ever go so wrong? Now we have a winter to rebuild our nest, then a spring to celebrate in. I never believed the sun would come out again.

Oh, by the way, Nina says the previous owner's wife

25

loathed Amanda. Much competition over the garden, apparently. Ah-man-dah always had to have the most exotic varieties of whatever, or things given to her by glamorous friends. Nina swears she sits in the garden of No 10 in summer playing the violin naked. What, I wonder? Airs on a G-spot? Pretentious twit. I shall *not* tell Harry though.

I've developed a theory about gardens – front gardens, that is. That they're people's spiritual washing, their souls hung out for the world to see. Let me take you down the street and show you what I mean. No 2 – next to us – is Kevin, the flashy film director. I've sussed him out now: the blonde who shook her hair at Harry is *not* his wife, as I suspected, or maybe she was the 'wife' of the week. There *is* apparently a real one, mostly in the country somewhere with the children. She believes he works terribly hard in London and only occasionally turns up so as not to disturb him. She certainly would; the turnover of busty blondes is as regular as the milkman. I see them leaving early in the morning in their designer jeans and high-heeled boots. They all have legs that go on for ever, and Kevin's appetite for them seems to go on for ever too (I wonder if his prick does. Nina refers to it as his Cruise missile). But the front garden; well, there you are, you can't see it at all because he's built a six-foot wall. A garden of well-advertised secrets.

No 3 is 'Arold the builder. His wife's a midget who looks like Minnie Mouse on springs and is desperately keen to be 'naice'. The Mercedes takes up most of the front garden, but Minnie's kept one area sacred. The shrine consists of plastic Greek amphorae arranged close to a pond with fibreglass nymphs desporting round a fountain. Harry refers to it as 'Versailles' and has dubbed it the 'Fontaine des Naffs'.

Our Scottish doctor is at No 4. No nonsense here. The front garden is tarmac for his-and-hers Ford Escorts, side by side. Dedicated servants of the NHS, though Nina tells me women won't go to his surgery during the winter because he always makes them strip to the waist, even if it's a bunion. My God, he must get an eyeful with Nina.

No 5 is Roger the historian, with the alcoholic nympho wife and a rather beautiful son who is mostly away at university. There's nothing at all in their front garden except an enormous tree with a preservation order on it, which seems to say it all in view of her predilections. But the tree takes all the light from No 6, where Mrs Courtenay Gascoigne parks her multiple prams and festoons the gravel with nappies daily. She's a serious breeder – no truck with disposable Pampers. (So there are two scrubbers next door to one another: don't you like that?)

After that there's Bill and Nina. One of the things I like about Nina is how she's made a front garden that totally contradicts Bill's house. Inside it's all domestic high-tec and gadgetry. Outside it's a wilderness, looks as though it might be a pocket-sized reserve for some endangered butterfly, though Nina assures me it's a mass of bluebells and wild daffodils in the spring. I asked her if the contrast was deliberate. 'Yes,' she said, 'I like to rough Bill up a bit,' and she laughed. She was wearing incredibly tight jeans; I'm glad Harry wasn't there.

27

Only three more to go. No 8's the whackiest. Louisa's the portrait painter's wife, the mystic freak who hands me literature and wears dung-coloured maxi-skirts extremely hand-woven. Her front garden is a place of earnest spiritual significance. There are two things in it: a hawthorn tree, (Joseph of Aramathea?), propped like an aged cripple on crutches; and a life-size carving of a figure (sex indeterminate) raising its arms to the heavens. Nina refers to it as, 'Woman adjusting shower-curtain', and now I can't think of it as anything else.

Am I boring you, Ruth, or are you enjoying this as much as I am? You'd love No 9. He's Maurice, some sort of advertising mogul who roars off early in the morning in his Jaguar, very handsome in a nasty way. But she's the most depressed creature you've ever seen. Actually rather beautiful behind the permanently downcast appearance. She's forever apologising, and you find yourself asking what for, which makes her apologise again for having to tell you. Then the tension-lines begin to crinkle at the corner of her mouth. Oh dear! Her name's Lottie. I think I'm going to have to take her in hand. I'll get her pissed one day and find out what's going on, or most certainly not going on, at least not with her. As for the front garden: empty, empty, empty. Except for the wilted remains of three cabbages. I pass by almost every day and think of that wilted life, and how it could have been mine. I feel a wave of sadness, and I feel anger. When tears are shed so publicly is it despair or self-congratulation? Supposing I lent Lottie *The Female Eunuch*: I can just hear her give a little sigh and say, 'Yes, of course, but what can I do? I've got the children to think of.' The excuse is always the children, isn't it?

And now on to No 10, the flamboyant Amanda, she of the violin and the heaving bosom. I've told you about Ah-man-dah. I hardly need to describe her front garden to you but I will – taking it calmly from the left. Let me see if I can do it properly like those arty programmes on telly. The eye perceives first of all an exquisite parterre of stones and raked gravel *à la japonaise*. (That's the mood bit.) Then follows an enchanted forest of bonsai trees, each writhing in miniature agony. And if you navigate this adventure there's the life-saving refreshment of the sunken garden, tiled by courtesy of the Alhambra, with a circular pool vivid with ornamental carp. (How am I doing? Oh, by the way, there's a heronry nearby which takes heavy toll of these delicacies, apparently.) That's not quite all – and this will rather spoil the artistic impression – because on the right-hand side is a large muslin sack growing on a stalk. I enquired delicately of Amanda the meaning of this unusual feature. She explained in ringing accents that it was a flowering tree of some important oriental origin which needed protection from the W4 climate. Didn't it rather defeat the purpose, having it buried in a sack? I suggested cattily. Oh no, she assured me, in April all would be revealed, and the scent, my darling, is *divine*. 'Doesn't it get vandalised?', I asked. And she demonstrated a special alarm-system with sirens and concealed lighting directly connected to the local police station. I said I was surprised it wasn't Kew, and she looked rather cross.

I'm afraid I've burbled on, so I'll wind up this saga and – Christ! I must go shopping. The mural's nearly finished. Bill (the architect) is very sweet about it. Teases me because I'm always singing while I paint. I've decided he's really rather attractive. Nina says he's good in bed.

Enough for now. Wheeee! I'm happy.

Love. Love. Love.

Janice.

PS Re-reading this, I begin to wonder about myself. Have you noticed how women in their thirties get released into vulgarity? That's me.

J.

November

69 Damaskinou
Neapolis
Athens

November 7th

Dear Janice,

We are not to be outdone – as you see, we too
have a place to call our own. But look how I'm
jinxed: I am fated to live at addresses that remind me
of previous postings I'd much rather forget. Damaskinou
presumably has something to do with Damascus (unless
of course he's a famously unknown Greek philosopher
– there are so many of them). As for No 69, the less said
the better, even to you.

Anyway, if you remember Athens you'll know that
the Neapolis district is the shabbier side of Mount
Lycabettos, the posh side being Kolonaki where our
ambassador lives along with ship-owners, Arab terrorists, the mistresses of most of the Greek cabinet and
the entire staff of those embassies whose governments
actually pay their diplomats a living wage. The Brits have
to make do with the scrag-end of town. However, at least

it's close to the archaeological museum which is a joy at this time of year, when the backpackers and the guided sheep have gone home and the guards are almost civil, though not always awake.

This city does not improve with acquaintance, but Piers and I are negotiating for a weekend country pad to rent, inland from the Gulf of Corinth in the hills. Only the meanest of shacks with no water, but it means that Piers can do his English eccentric bit and potter about in knee-length shorts looking for rare anemones and insignificant orchids. I shall *not* garden or collect garish local weaving, I assure you. I shall read improving books like Marquez and Updike, and get drunk. And when I'm bored with these and with Piers I intend to travel. In fact I shall probably travel a lot, since I get bored with Piers easily and improving books always give me a wanderlust by making me feel I know hopelessly little about the greater world. The trouble is, when I travel I take with me the most *un*improving books and hurry back convinced I'd rather be bored by Piers than read them. In short, I'm a wilful dilettante with no intention of changing.

Now, you asked me some heavy questions about marriage, open and closed etc. After all these years you ask me! How very earnest you are sometimes. I wish I could think of a suitable quotation and just hand it to you to make what you can of it. Do I tell Piers everything? No, of course not. He may be cool but he's not a block of ice. I tell him when it doesn't matter, or when I can make a joke of it – sex can be hilariously funny in retrospect – or when I know it'll turn him on. That's a bonus, like watching a video when it's *you* in there. Sometimes he does the same and I get wildly jealous and randy. What I'm saying, Janice, is that you have to feel terribly safe to play games like that. And I do. But I also know I'd wither away if I could never make love again to anyone except my husband. It would be like being condemned to eat hamburger and chips for the rest of my life. (No, Piers is more like steak tartare.) By Ruth's law, marriage has to be an artful compromise, and the art is half the fun of it.

Does any of that make sense to you? I'm revelling in your account of life in 'Coronation Street' – so many peas in a pod (don't you sometimes feel like shelling them?) I like the sound of Nina, and your garden psychology is spot on. I notice, however, that you don't include plans for your own garden. Perhaps I should do it for you, and you tell me if I'm right. The sobering thing is that I couldn't. Is this because I don't really know you at all? That may be true. After all, I never imagined you'd get hitched to Harry in the first place. I never thought you'd kick him out after twelve years, and I never dreamed you'd try again. So what's the next surprise?

When you've had your winter of nest-building, do please come to Greece in the spring and we'll go on the spree.

Love from the concrete jungle,

Ruth.

ATHENS 1200 HRS NOVEMBER 10
CABLE DESPATCH TO:
JANICE BLAKEMORE
1 RIVER MEWS LONDON W4 UK
TRIED PHONING BACK UNSUCCESSFULLY
STOP HAVE CANCELLED TRIP COME
SOONEST COMFORT TEARS ALCOHOL
STOP SOD HARRY RAGE RAGE STOP RUTH

My dearest Ruth,

Felt a lot better after phoning you yesterday. Sorry I screamed and yelled – just had to – and then your sweet telegram arrived in the evening (spent alone – I couldn't bear to be with Harry even though the bastard offered to stay in, all quiet and sheepish. Of course part of me wanted him here, and that made it worse). So I watched television – everything, anything, pictures and voices, the late film, God knows what it was, it seemed as meaningless as I was. I even slept a bit on the sofa, then made myself coffee around dawn this morning and walked along the river till I knew H would have left. Lovely grey river, the Thames waking with ducks and gliding swans following me beside the towpath. Why me? Did they think I was going to throw myself in? I even laughed. The worst bit was seeing ordinary life. Families having breakfast. Children leaving for school. I felt like a refugee.

It's midday now. I don't dare have a drink or

depression will hit me like a wave unless I drink so much that I just pass out – but think of the hangover I'd have as well. At the moment I feel numb, anaesthetised, almost bored by the thought that I've been through this so many, many times. This occasion seems worse and better than before. Worse because there were so many rekindled hopes, as you know, and so much reborn trust, all shattered now – so much of myself exposed and then thrown away. What a waste! And better because it's the last time. The last torture. I hear myself saying, 'You'll never have to go through this again. Never.' Like you said on the phone, it's the end of something rotten and soon there'll be the beginning of something good.

And that other thing you said, 'You don't *need* to love him.' I keep thinking of that. Can I stop loving him, just like that? And do you know, it was strange; after I put the phone down two lines of a John Donne poem came into my head as though they'd been waiting for me all these years: 'Love is a growing or full constant light, and his first minute after noon is night.' Yes, I know I don't need to love him. God I feel brave saying that; even as I'm writing I can feel great thumps of pain inside and I've got to keep writing in order to ward them off. At least writing I'm not alone; it proves I'm sort of sane, stringing words together. Perhaps I'll even try telling you how it happened. Yes, I shall. Here goes.

It was Tuesday, the day before yesterday. Harry was working at home and said he had to go into town for a while. Not long afterwards I went to Nina's house to add some final bits and pieces to Bill's mural. I'd bought some special colours. After about an hour I left to come home, and as I opened Nina's front door I saw Harry leave No 10 and walk quickly towards the river. We often walk to the Underground that way, and for a moment I didn't understand and almost called after him. Then it struck me; he'd been gone at least an hour and a half. So what the . . . ? I knew immediately. No 10 is Amanda's house. An hour and a half! Harry is having an affair with Amanda. Of course he is. He'd waited till her children were at school and her husband was at work, then went off down the road and into her bed.

All this time – no more than a few seconds probably – I was standing in the road clutching my painting things. My whole life had changed in those moments: it was as clear as if I'd just read it on one of those notices the council puts up on lampposts, 'Harry is screwing Amanda. Any objections to the above should be referred to the town clerk by . . .' Objections? I ran home and couldn't even cry. I stood staring at photos of Clive in his football gear, at a 'Welcome Home' card I'd sent Harry only a couple of months ago, and at the furniture we'd bought together just a few weeks ago; and I realised my hands hurt where I'd been gripping the back of a chair. When would Harry come back, I kept thinking. I had to see him, be told it wasn't true – there were a hundred good reasons why he might have been there – and he would laugh and everything would be all right, wouldn't it? Except that I knew it wasn't all right, that it never would be all right. That hurt so much I thought I'd collapse. So I rang Nina and told her everything. There was a long pause and then, oh Ruth, it was like a kick in the stomach, do you know what she said? 'Yes, I know.' And she said it so calmly, as if it was just one of life's little problems and I'd get used to it. Should I have hated her? I did. I just put the phone down. Then I went to the bathroom and was sick.

I felt more alone than I can ever remember. I phoned mother, just to speak to someone I'd known before I met Harry. Of course I didn't say anything, and she prattled away about something or other. When could she come up and see the new house? How was Clive's new school? Was there somewhere I could play tennis, wouldn't that be nice? And so on. I don't know what I said, but I wished I hadn't phoned.

Then I had a strange feeling. I didn't want to confront Harry. Not that day. I'm not sure if I was being cruel to him or to myself, but I wanted to keep my own horrible secret, and to see how he kept his. He came back at about seven, with whisky on his breath. Was that to disguise the perfume, I found myself wondering. I heard myself asking the usual banal questions: how's your day been? Have they put the Christmas decorations up in Regent Street already? And he made the usual replies. It seemed so easy for him to hide it. I was sure he'd been covering up like this for weeks. And I thought of Amanda's patronising remarks a little while ago, 'Darling, you've got such pretty hair,' and, 'Harry's so good at his job, you must be proud of him.' Good at his job? Shit! Was he good in bed with her? *I* never found him so particularly, but perhaps that was because he was never thinking of me, just saving it up until he could tear off all those ethnic garments and bury his face in the heaving bosom.

I'd forgotten all about supper – hadn't eaten anything all day. He seemed surprised, but only a little. Shrugged his shoulders, read the evening paper, then a bit later wandered off and made himself some scrambled eggs. Didn't say anything except just once, 'Aren't you hungry?' We watched telly for a while. Then I knew I couldn't sleep in the same bed as him. This would have been the moment to say something – or should have been. But I wanted to keep my secret a bit longer. I just said I felt like staying up for a while and, 'Why don't you go off to bed?' He shrugged again and said good-night. I snatched bits of sleep where I was in the chair in front of the box. The telly closed down and I never bothered to turn it off. It hummed through the night, then began again with soft morning music. I felt worse and wished I'd confronted him already.

Suddenly I felt furious. I got a bucket from the kitchen, filled it with cold water and threw it in his face as he lay sleeping. Then I rushed downstairs and out of the house. There was a coffee bar open in the high street and I found myself eating toast and marmalade as if nothing had happened. It was Golden Shred, and I remember thinking it ought to have been Cooper's Oxford. I wanted to stay there gazing at people walking to work, the street waking up, confident young men coming out of the cold rubbing their hands, dolly-birds being flirted with by the Italian café-owner over the expresso machine, a balding man poring over 'Page Three'. A young man sat himself opposite me and smiled: very good-looking, probably ten years younger than me. 'On your way to work?', he asked. He meant, 'Where do you work, and why don't you have a drink with me afterwards?' I felt flattered and half-wished he'd ask me, but then I got a whiff of his aftershave. And as I got up to leave, there was Harry. He didn't look angry, only anxious. 'I've been looking for you everywhere. Please, let's talk.' I was shaking my head. There was nothing to talk about. 'I know about everything,' I said, 'It's just the same as ever, isn't it?' He was saying, 'No, it isn't,' and I got angry. 'Why don't you just fuck off?' Everyone in the café stared at us.

We were walking home. He was a few paces behind, silent. I opened the door and slammed it in his face. Bolted it. He rang a few times, then sloped off. I began to regret not letting him talk, and nearly ran after him. Then I began to cry. I thought I'd never stop. I don't know how long it went on for, but that was when I phoned you.

Ruth, what should I do? Is there anything I can do? Should I go and see a solicitor, put the house back on the market, move into a temporary flat, and then what? Clive will be coming home for Christmas. Oh darling, that tears me apart. I want to curl into a ball and sleep for ever.

I must make myself think, think, think. I WILL NOT BE WRETCHED. There *will* be a life for me – I shall make it. And I'll ring, and write again very soon, and maybe come to Greece before Clive's holidays. It's sweet of you to wait for me.

With so much love,

Janice.

1 *River Mews*

November 12th

Clive darling,

Of course you can stay with your friend before Christmas: how extremely kind of his mother. You mean they actually *own* part of Exmoor? Goodness me. So what will you do, come back here first at the end of term – around December 15th, isn't it – and then go and spend a week there? (Don't get snowed in for Christmas, whatever you do.) I should be able to drive you down; Daddy's likely to be in Bucharest around then, he says – in fact he'll probably be going there quite soon – but he'll be back for Christmas, of course.

The new house is coming along and we've got some new furniture for the sitting-room. I've met the boy at No 10 I told you about, but frankly I don't think you're going to want to play with him. He's a bit stuck up (his mother too) and goes to some horribly posh school. In any case you'll have your old schoolmates around, won't you?

I don't think there's any other news to speak of except that I've finished the big painting our new friends at No 7 asked me to do. I'll take you round to see it when you're home – which won't be long now. I'm so looking forward to it, as is Daddy.

All my love to you, darling.

Mummy.

1 River Mews
London W4

November 13th

Dear Piers,

I wanted to drop you a line before leaving for Bucharest tomorrow – probably for a month, or longer if the present turmoil in Romania continues. In theory, reporting should be a lot easier post-Ceausescu, and what I see and hear may actually bear some resemblance to the truth at last. My suspicion, though, is that familiar Western delusions will still apply; i.e., flocks of scavenger reporters arriving with democratic conceptions of black-and-white, only to discover that the new goodies in white hats differ little from the old baddies in black hats, and today's liberators are already half-way to being tomorrow's tyrants. I'm promised a Romanian guide-cum-interpreter who will turn out to be fuck-all use in Timosoara where they speak Hungarian anyway, and even less use in other parts of the country where they speak languages no one hitherto knew existed. But that's the name of the game, and very soon I shall have had a surfeit of Aids babies, disenfranchised minorities, loony ideologues and limp churchmen. After so many years of print journalism, TV reporting seems miraculously brief – three urgent sentences uttered in front of a burnt-out tank and then, 'This is Harry Blakemore, ITN, Bucharest'.

How serene your diplomatic life sounds. You're very funny about the social merry-go-round in Athens; I always imagined such goings-on to be the invention of English novelists whose sources of information were other English novelists. It was indiscreet of you in the extreme to relate quite so many details of your Prime Minister's love-life – I am after all a reporter and may hold you at gun-point one day. Needless to say I enjoyed every word of it, and only wish I could be with you in the cradle of corruption rather than squelching around among the Slavic hordes.

You say Ruth found herself a toyboy in the Peloponnese. Well, lack of enterprise was never her weakness, nor indeed yours, though I should have thought the First Secretary to Her Britannic Majesty's ambassador to the Hellenes might have secured himself a secretary who didn't resemble Joyce Grenfell on the hockey field. Your own stormproof marriage is an enviable contrast to my own, I have to say. Here I've managed to incur the wrath of Hurricane Janice – entirely my own fault, but none the more restful for that. I allowed myself some freeplay recently with an intriguing creature down the road, who made herself abundantly available on the very first acquaintance – and abundance is the word. Of course it was unforgivable and treacherous under the circumstances and I feel duly mortified. But as you know, I've never been one to say no to a good offer, and as always I didn't even think about it: a one-afternoon stand, that was all. Then unexpectedly it got a bit out of hand. It's not only that the woman is truly wonderful in bed. What shook me was that I discovered a warmth and gentleness with her which I realise I've always looked for and have never been able to find with Janice. So it became a sort of lifeline. When I'm with Amanda I'm a different person; a lot nicer. There's a kind of harmony between us, ease, a naturalness. We love and laugh. Nothing's false, nothing's held back. I'm none of those things with Janice. We came back together with the most sincere of intentions and a determination to begin again, and yet within a few days it was precisely the same as before. Tensions. Evasions. Pretences. Headaches. The sighs of do-hurry-up-darling. My fault? Her fault? Chemistry? Who knows? At the same time I love her. That's the paradox. What a mess, andI don't know how to get out of it.

Anyway, she found out and tipped a bucket of water over me in bed, which showed spirit. Nothing I say makes any difference – after all, what can I say? Now we're not speaking, and frankly I can't wait to get away, even to Romania. The old escape route. I'm afraid I'm no good at being married. If I meet an attractive woman I want to go to bed with her. I just like it. It's the way I am. Being a lover suits me – just the best of two people together, the grot left

48

behind. On the other hand it never suits women, does it? Christ, Amanda already announces she wants to leave her husband and marry me. But then it would start all over again. Who knows, I might find myself having an affair with Janice, and it might work a treat. Ridiculous, isn't it?

So, all's not at all quiet on the Western front. I wish Janice and I could somehow live like you and Ruth. Absolute fidelity should *not* be a condition of commitment. Sex is a rogue elephant and cannot be corralled.

Ah well!

Yours in the dog-house,

Harry.

1 River Mews

November 14th

Darling Clive,

Daddy left for Romania today. There's been a revolution of sorts there and he's got to see what's going on and report back. You may see his face on television if Mr Barlow allows you to watch the news.

So I'm on my own. It's horribly like old times, but I shall find plenty to do. On Saturday I have my 'junk' stall in Acton, and after that it's still possible I may go and visit Ruth in Athens for a week if I can find a friend to feed Spindle, the new kitten. I hope you like her – she's fluffy and all black except for white paws, as though she's just tiptoed through one of my paint pots.

Our next door neighbour – the film director called Kevin – had an all-night party last night, so I'm exhausted. It was quite impossible to sleep for the noise. All the other neighbours are furious, and Tilly (who's a doctor) at No 4 is drawing up some sort of petition. She's Scottish and very fierce. A heron's made off with all the goldfish in the pond at No 10, which I find rather funny. The silly woman was screaming about it in a flimsy nightdress this morning in her front garden – didn't seem to feel the cold, but then she's rather fat.

Keep well, my darling. See you soon.

All my love,

Mummy.

Oh Janice darling,

I've been wondering what I could possibly say to you after your phone call last week. Then your letter arrived this morning and you sounded a whole lot calmer. 'I will not be wretched': I like the defiance of that.

You're right of course; you mustn't be wretched. Jealousy is the worst of things, isn't it, because it destroys the will to act – except perhaps to kill the bitch, which you might try if you've got a good alibi. You know, you're a lovely person; you're intelligent and kind, a bit too kind; you're incredibly pretty – that short blonde hair and blue eyes, stunning, envy-making; you've got a Botticelli figure, and there's not a man with anything between his ears or legs who wouldn't fancy you like crazy. (Piers does, as you well know.) By the way, Harry's been writing to Piers and is apparently contrite and wallowing in self-pity. The usual rubbish. If feckless men need to deceive themselves, why do they have to do it in clichés? He talks about it being his 'nature', and he can't help it though he'd like to. The same old crap: the woman did tempt me and I did eat.

Well, I don't know about *your* nature, sweetheart, but mine would now be telling me to kick the arsehole out for good. It's not the infidelity so much (I'm no one to talk); it's the deception. If Harry wants to wave his prick at everyone who gives him the glad-eye, then he should stop pretending to be Goodie-Two-Shoes. Janice, you don't need me to tell you, the man's a first-rate shit. Of course some women deserve first-rate shits – lots of women in fact, doormats, Florence Nightingales, mother superiors – but you're not one of them. You're loving and loyal and deserve better than that.

Oh God, now *I'm* thinking in clichés. Why is it that there are hundreds of witty and original ways of being bitchy, but sympathy always comes in brand names? Now I'm going to be positive and wise: are you ready? Throw him out – end of Volume One of your life. Have a decent (brief) period of distress. Then begin to see as many people as you can, committing yourself to *none* of them and preferably sleeping with none of them (too early, too dangerous). Finally come out here in the spring as we originally planned, bringing with you a couple of slinky dresses and some excellent perfume, and leave the rest to me.

How's that for a life-plan? Well, a short-term life-plan?

Courage, ma brave. Try and get through Christmas as best you can, and next summer I'll come over for the Wimbledon tennis fortnight and we'll go to the Centre Court on my debenture tickets – lots of times.

Love,

Ruth.

PS Piers is learning Greek. It's a hoot! It transforms his

personality. He throws his arms about and gets cross when I laugh. His tutor's taken a shine to me – wants to teach me, too. I tell him there's not much he could, and he looks embarrassed. I can see the worrybeads will be out in force before long.

PPS The weekend pad's heavenly. There'll be electricity and water by the spring, all ready for your trysts. You wait, you wait!

R.

1 River Mews

November 23rd

My dearest Ruth,

I'm not sure if I should laugh or cry. Let me start by telling you that things have happened, and I am not the person you thought I was, or that *I* thought I was.

Step by step. Yesterday (before I got your 'wise' letter – for which thank you) I woke up miserable and angry. Another grey dawn, kitten to feed, breakfast telly, housework, Harry a thousand miles away, Clive at school: what on earth was I doing here? Eventually I told myself, 'Think positively, Janice.' So I tried to think positively. The moment I made that brave decision who should I see teetering past but the sweet-smelling Ah-man-dah, all doozied-up and clearly out to dazzle the world. I went outside to have another look and cursed her for having good legs. At the same time I noticed that Robert the husband's car was still outside No 10. Then it came to me – I wonder what he has to say about his wife's carryings-on. Let's find out. I felt a surge of delicious malice: I'll have a really good stir.

By the time I got to the door of No 10 I'd made myself hopping mad, and gave a sharp kick at the horrible wrapped tree on the way. Actually I was terrified, but stoked up the anger to hide it. I rang the bell. Robert opened the door looking perplexed. I'm not sure he even knew who I was, this little blonde calling on him. He had his glasses on and was obviously working. All the same he was extremely courteous and asked me in – wasn't I Janice from down the road? What could he do? Would I like some coffee? Sorry, Amanda was out.

Well, I'd hardly noticed him before: rather a flustered man he seemed, going a bit bald on top, fortyish, tall, rather anaemic-looking, but a sensitive face – chiselled – with a shy smile. I was surprised to feel at ease with him and my anger began to evaporate. Instead of blurting it all out I asked him quite calmly, did he know Amanda and my Harry were having an affair – in his own house and presumably in his own bed? I couldn't tell much from his face, and anyway I was now in full flow. I thought it was not on, I said (what a mild way of putting it). I wasn't blaming him of course, I explained; presumably he was as innocent as I was. It was mostly Harry's fault, the bastard – thank God he was in Bucharest; but what did he think about his wife waiting till the coast was clear and then leaping into bed with another man? And what did he think should be done about it? I sounded so morally indignant I felt I should have added, 'Tut tut!'

There was a heavy silence for a few moments, and I noticed his hands were shaking as he held his coffee cup. I felt amazingly calm now that I'd had my say. Calm with virtue. I even felt quite sorry for him. He kept starting to say things and stopping with a gulp. Finally he put his head in his hands with his elbows on the table, and I think he was trying not to cry. I wanted to hold his hand – ridiculous, isn't it? 'It's not easy with Amanda,' he said eventually. 'She's . . .' But he didn't finish. 'Does she have a lot of affairs?', I asked, feeling rather crude. But I wanted to know.

He shook his head and said 'No! No! Not really, but . . .' And again he didn't finish. I knew I didn't need to ask him what the 'but' meant. The story of his marriage was all over his face. I found myself liking him. It was strangely comforting to be there, and I told him about Harry and me – it all came blurting out – about the separation, about his infidelities. I even told him about the bucket of water I threw over him, and he laughed. Ruth, I felt happy being able to talk to him – two innocent parties sharing our pain. He was quite at ease by now, and seemed relieved that I wasn't raging and screaming. He admitted it had been like this with Amanda for quite a few years. They'd married young, much too young. Then there were the children. Now they didn't make love any more. No agreement about it: they just didn't. She never even undressed in front of him. He had affairs too, sometimes, but casually, mostly when he was away filming, and they didn't count for anything. He still loved Amanda, he said. He still fancied her. She was a bit special. Then he asked me – did I still love Harry? I think he was hoping I'd say yes.

Ruth, I heard myself say, 'No!' I really did. And I meant it. I told him I didn't think I wanted to love anyone at all; at least not like that, not totally. I wanted to be free, and free to be happy. I thought it sounded banal as I said it, but he was shaking his head again and looking down at the table. 'You're right,' he was saying. 'That's what I'd like to be, too – free to be happy. I'm glad you're here,' he added after a moment. There was an odd silence, and he got up to pour some coffee to break it. I didn't want any coffee and said perhaps I ought to be going: I'd interrupted him from working, hadn't I? 'Don't,' he said. 'Not yet.' And then he stretched out a hand and started to undo the buttons of my blouse, slowly, deliberately. There were lots of them, and he just went on and on. I did absolutely nothing, and he seemed to know that I wouldn't. I felt like a fruit being carefully peeled, and it was incredibly exciting. Finally there I was, and he laid both hands over my breasts. Well, that was it. I closed my eyes. I remember saying, 'Please, not in your bed,' knowing that Harry had been there. We made love on the floor. It was amazing. The sheer hunger. We did things I've never done. I did things I didn't know I knew. And it went on and on – like getting drunk and then getting drunk again.

When I finally got dressed I said to myself, 'I've just been fucked stupid.' The strange thing was, as I left I couldn't see why I'd desired him. I couldn't believe I had. He seemed very ordinary. It was as if I'd never done it. He wanted to kiss me and I just gave him a peck on the cheek.

Ruth, what's going on? I feel a million dollars. It's been twelve years. I've never been unfaithful, and it was so easy! Ridiculous. It's as if all sorts of chains have fallen away. Am I a new woman? Am I liberated? I'm certainly liberated from Amanda in one fell swoop; the fat cow, I no longer care about her at all. Nor about Harry much. I got out of my bath this morning and looked at myself in the mirror. That's really pretty neat, I thought. Botticelli figure, you said. Venus floating in among rose petals. Robert said I had much nicer breasts than Amanda. Champagne-cup-sized. I bet hers droop, all stretch-marks.

Ruth, I know I'll absolutely never make love to him again.

Does all this surprise you? And where on earth do I go from here?

From your good little Protestant friend, in amazement, and with love and laughter,

Janice.

Dear Janice,

I've begun half a dozen letters to you and torn them
up. Now I'm trying again, but clear thinking isn't helped
by this place, where nothing is as it seems and hard news
has a habit of melting into fantasy even as I report it. I
don't know if you've been tuning in to any of my news
reports – you probably switch off in anger – but if so
you will have seen a journalist grasping at straws.

Nobody really knows what's going on here, not
even those supposedly in the know. As far as I can
see, the international press corps spends much of its
time interviewing national 'saviours', who turn out next
day to be Securitate officers trying to save their skins.
Corruption is more than a way of life in Romania, it's
a religion. And it rains, it rains.

I got out into the countryside yesterday with my
interpreter and tried to speak to some peasants in villages
that Ceausescu had been in the process of bulldozing.
The look on their faces was one of blank suspicion – years
of knowing no one could be trusted, especially people
like me who say, 'Trust me.' I got one whiskered old boy
to talk a bit about conditions since the revolution, and
then as the interpreter was relaying what he said a voice
in the crowd yelled out in English, 'That's not what the
man said at all.' So even my interpreter lies. How shall

I find one who doesn't? Kafka didn't die, he just moved to Romania.

But I love this job, hopeless though it may be. I feel stretched, demanded of, witness to an agonising struggle for rebirth. The journalist here finds himself in the role of incompetent midwife.

Perhaps I'm deliberately avoiding what I really need to write to you about, which is my behaviour of course – mainly – but it's also the way we relate to one another, or fail to. You may never want me back, and I accept that, but there are things I need to explain, and try to put to you honestly.

I know that the way I behave is out of despair over what we don't seem capable of achieving – or when we do it doesn't last. I really thought it would last this time, and then after a while the old familiar tensions began to return and I don't understand why. There was that evening a few weeks ago when you looked particularly lovely and I wanted to undress you, but you put your hands across your chest and turned away. I felt hurt and rejected. Janice, I so much want a life of ease and harmony with you, to be able to love and make love to you without barriers of suspicion. Is it me? If so, tell me what I do, or don't do. Sometimes the atmosphere is so tense it's like living in a minefield. I can feel your unhappiness and I can feel my own. That's when I go away from you. I know it's weak of me, but when I'm miserable I seek comfort.

What I absolutely promise is that Amanda means nothing to me at all. It was a one-off. There's been nobody else. It's you I want, and want to be able to love. You and Clive matter more to me than anything in the world. You know, I look around this place where everything has been wrecked, and I tell myself how lucky I am. We have a chance. Please let's take it. Let's try again. Let Christmas be a time of healing.

I love you so much, and need you, my beautiful girl.

Harry.

December

Hotel Ganymede
Galaxidi
Greece

December 1st

Dear Janice,

You seem to have recovered all too quickly, my
brazen hussy. Good for you. This is just a jotting
between gin and tonics (in the hotel garden, would
you believe it, on the 1st of December?) to say that
since you're obviously *not* going to descend on me as a
stretcher case I decided to come here after all (heavenly
place – recommend) for a couple of days as a base for
exploring Delphi.

More when I get back to Athens. But I certainly
shan't waste any more advice on you.

Piers has piles. Romantic, isn't it?

Huge love,

Ruth.

December 6th

My dearest Ruth,

I'm in the most awful need. God, I wish you were here to help me and keep me sane. Actually I'm a lot calmer than I was, and I shall try to remain extremely cool and tell you about it.

On Monday I heard from Harry in Bucharest. Being a good journalist he writes good letters, rather too good – I've become wary of his literary sweet-talk. True to form, the letter disturbed me; Harry knows exactly which bruises to press and which sweeteners to hold out. There was a good deal of *mea culpa* – it was all on account of our relationship, he feels rejected. Then a dig or two at me for being frigid (no recollection of that myself), and finally a tearful assurance that the business with Amanda was simply a 'one-off', and it's me he loves, let's try again.

I felt like pulp and just sat there at the breakfast table crying. I didn't believe him and yet I wanted to. If only it were really true. How wonderful *not* to have to go through the mess of divorce, solicitors, splitting assets, ('Is that your picture or mine?'), having to explain it all to Clive, having to take endless phone calls, ('No, Harry's not here I'm afraid'). And then just the prospect of being alone, and frightened of being alone. I hated those six months of it – I was only half of myself, the rest numb – and to think that could be for the rest of my life. Growing old and grey *alone*!

So I sat there for ages. Could I really take him back *again*? God, I so wished he hadn't written! All my reserves, carefully collected together, were broken into little pieces around me. I felt like a smashed doll.

Then the phone went and it was Nina. I hadn't quite forgiven her for being so callous about the No 10 business but it was a bright, sunny morning and she suggested a game of tennis on the public courts opposite. I hadn't played for ages but it's something I've missed, and anyway I needed company, so I agreed. Being winter, the courts were empty and it turned out to be great fun. Nina's better than me but more than a little handicapped by her frontage – when she runs for the ball it's like two boyscouts fighting in a sack. I couldn't help laughing. I was mean and kept trying to play the ball at her feet where I was pretty sure she couldn't see it. She beat me anyway, but I did almost take a set off her before blisters and general exhaustion took over.

As we walked back I felt rosy-cheeked and healthy. I suggested we play regularly. Nina agreed and asked me in for a drink. I glanced at my mural in Bill's study and felt proud. He loved it, Nina assured me. She opened a bottle of Chardonnay and we sat by her window, drinking it in the sun. A couple of glasses and I knew I needed to talk about Harry. So I told her about the letter – what Harry had said about me, what he said about Amanda, and about wanting to try again.

I'm not sure what I needed her to say. Nothing, probably. Just to listen and be sympathetic, and let me talk my way through to an answer. I could feel my eyes filling with tears again, and the wine didn't help. Nina sat impassively in her tennis outfit, and as I talked I became conscious of odd things – her heavy hands wrapped round the glass, the mole on her cheek, the sweat stains round her armpits. I made a guess at what size bra she must take, which made me conscious that I never wear one, and I wondered if she was thinking that too. It even occurred to me that she might be lesbian – it was something about the way she was gazing at me. Curious, isn't it, how you can be talking terribly seriously and still have quite different thoughts at the same time. Or is it just me?

I realised I must have mentioned to her at least three times that the Amanda business was just a one-off according to Harry. Why do I keep referring to it as 'business'? Is it because I don't like to think of them in bed together? Suddenly she stopped me. 'Look,' she said, and poured us both another glass of wine, 'there's something you should probably know.' I felt myself go cold. There was that same calm in her voice as when she told me she'd known about Harry and Amanda all along. 'He's been phoning and writing to her. Amanda told me, and it doesn't sound like a one-off.' There was a pause that felt like a chasm – does everyone tell fucking Nina everything? 'He's asked her to join him out there, and they're planning holidays, weekends.'

I wonder if I'd have felt better if Nina had put her arms round me. I wanted her to – I wanted to cry like a baby – but she didn't. She just sat there sipping her wine. I wanted to ask her how she could tell me things like that and then offer me no comfort at all. Nothing. I was trapped. I couldn't just leave, or perhaps I could have but didn't anyway. There was another awful silence. I spilt my wine and Nina went into the kitchen to fetch a cloth.

While she was gone I tried to pull myself together. So now I knew. That was it. I thought of Harry's letter which had arrived just that morning. So sincere, gushing with it; that was the worst part, that he *meant* it all. Something I'd never realised before is that the most dangerous liars are the ones who believe their own lies.

Nina came back into the room and poured the last trickle of wine into my glass. I felt as though I was in the sick-room being treated by matron.

Then I mumbled something like, 'Oh well'. Nina sat down again by the window and was gazing out into the garden. Then she said suddenly, 'It's just about appetites, isn't it?' Can you believe it? Appetites! Good God! I tried to say that I thought it was about a lot of other things too – like trust, promises, loyalty, not letting people down, not letting your *wife* down. And would you believe it? Nina laughed. A small, dismissive laugh. 'You really shouldn't take it all so much to heart, Janice,' she went on. 'It's only sex. It won't last. It never does. Sex gets boring after a while. Don't you find that? I certainly do.'

Ruth, I always thought I was a gentle soul. Not any more I don't. I was livid. 'I certainly *don't*!', I yelled at her. 'I love being fucked and I want to go on being fucked, and what's more, if I have a regular lover I don't expect to share him with some floozie down the road. If

I'm free, then I'll bloody well fuck whoever I choose, but if I'm committed to someone I'm committed to him, I'm his and I want him to be mine!'

It was quite a speech, I can tell you. I surprised myself. I know you don't agree, but you would have been proud of me none the less.

That wasn't nearly the end of it, though. Nina opened another bottle of wine. I rather wished she hadn't. 'Come on, you're upset,' was all she said. Upset! Of course I was bloody upset. I was enraged. For a moment I wondered if I might blurt out about Robert and me and how we'd screwed on the floor of Amanda's house; I knew it would have gone straight back to the old cow and that would have tickled me. But then of course it would have gone straight back to Harry, and I want to appear squeaky-clean in that direction, at least for the time being. So I said nothing and silently fumed.

I remember the last bit of the conversation painfully well. After so coolly pronouncing me 'upset', Nina suggested I really didn't have too much to worry about, because with my looks I wouldn't find it hard to get another man if that was what I wanted. Christ, I'd just had some of the most miserable weeks of my entire life and she was talking as if it was no more than trading in a car for a newer model! I replied rather bitchily that with her tits I didn't imagine she'd have much trouble either. And do you know what she said? 'Yes, your Harry rather fancied them.' 'You mean to say . . . ?', I gulped. She paused just long enough to make me convinced she was about to lie. 'As a matter of fact, no,' she said. 'I tend to prefer men less available than that. Anyway, it's not me.'

I felt battered and about two inches high. 'Very decent of you,' I said sourly. She just looked at me, and I could see she was weighing up something in her mind. Then she got up and stood by the window. I felt even smaller and utterly miserable. What was she going to say next? What more could she say?

I didn't have to wait very long. She cleared her throat like an after-dinner speaker. 'You think I'm hard, don't you? But what's hard for me, Janice,' she went on, 'is knowing things you don't know that maybe you ought to know, because everyone else does.' I could feel myself freeze inside again. 'Your Harry's made a pass at just about every woman in this street. It isn't just Amanda. It's Lottie at No 9. Certainly Roger's wife at No 5, the drunk. Courtenay's wife. Me. God knows which of Kevin's innumerable bimbos he's managed to hijack. He seems to go in for big women.' There was still room for that one to hurt. 'I don't know how many he's managed to screw, probably not that many. Then finally he found Amanda. Altogether quite a performance in however long it is since you moved in. I'd have thought you're better off without him, don't you?'

I didn't even have the strength to ask, 'How do you know all this?' It was just about the worst moment of my life. Nina half-carried me back to the house.

Oh Harry, I wonder if you know what you've lost? I've loved you and wanted to be with you all my life. That was all I wanted. I used to think about growing old with you, holding hands as the darkness gathered. Dying with you. Was it really too much to ask that you should feel the same about me? Why did you marry me

69

if you knew you couldn't? And why did you ever come back? Why did you have to torment me?

Ruth, I feel abandoned and humiliated, and I don't know what to do. I hate Harry and I hate this place – this street, with its greed, complacency and privileged cynics. I feel cheated, soiled, belittled. Sod them all, Harry and the rest of them! You know, I think I want to do something utterly outrageous to pay him back, pay them all back – and then leave and start my life again.

Any ideas?

Love from Rotten Row,

Janice.

1 River Mews

December 7th

Clive darling,

The sad news is that Daddy isn't going to be here for Christmas. I heard from him a couple of days ago and it seems he's tied up with other commitments. A shame. We'll just have to make it a super Christmas on our own. I'll get a big tree – one of those ones that doesn't shed its needles all over the carpet in five minutes. And we can decorate it together as soon as you're back from Exmoor.

I've taken up tennis again, with Nina down the road. The aches and blisters are killing me. If the weather keeps fine we might have a game, you and me. Help settle the Christmas pudding (which I've just made, by the way). The tennis court's next to the graveyard, so if I keel over it'll be convenient.

Spindle the kitten's growing fast and increasingly mischievous. She's taken to swinging from Daddy's dressing-gown behind the bedroom door and tugging long threads from it. Don't know why he didn't take it with him to Bucharest, but maybe he's found something else to keep him warm.

See you next week, my darling, and we'll have a lovely drive down to the West Country. There'll be lots to talk about. What's your friend's name? I ought to know, just in case his mother rings up to check if everything's all right. Perhaps you could phone me if you have a chance.

Glad the football's going well. And the singing. I love Christmas carols. Shall we go carol singing together?

All my love,

Mummy.

LONDON W4 1100 HRS DECEMBER 7
CABLE DESPATCH TO: BLAKEMORE
TRANSYLVANIA HOTEL BUCHAREST
ROMANIA
LYING BASTARD GO EFF YOURSELF STOP
GOODBYE STOP JANICE

My dear Janice,

I was going to write you a long letter about Delphi,
but after receiving yours I got the feeling that Delphic
orifices might be more appropriate than oracles. Forgive
the crudity, but as you rightly say, women become
more vulgar with age (and men more pompous, which
Piers, thank God, is not – boring sometimes, yes, but
pompous never).

Your letter was such a cry from the heart, my
dearest, I felt wounded for you and wanted to hop on
the next plane to be with you and hold your hand. What
to do? Well, there's nothing more to be said about Harry
Blakemore, ITN, Bucharest, is there? He's the sort of
man who convinces himself he can have it both ways
and will certainly end up with neither; then he'll bore
the pants off everyone with self-recrimination for the
rest of his life: 'She was too good for me'. Dead right,

she was. Of course you have to accept the possibility that Ah-man-dah's exactly the sort of twit he needs, and maybe they'll live happily ever after. But let that be no further concern of yours: he is absolutely not the man *you* need.

So, exit Harry – and now what? From your letter I can smell revenge in the air, and God how I sympathise. From the way you describe it your little street is a hotbed (sorry!) of all the furtive hypocrisies I despise most. Respectability is public, treachery is secret. Women are expected to keep a stiff upper lip and men a stiff upper cock (oh, here I go again). Nobody's supposed to disturb the social ethos, and the laws of the jungle are hidden behind immaculate front gardens. Even unhappiness is half-hearted, and nobody cares about anything deeply: it's all far less important than the children's expensive education and the monthly delivery from the Wine Society. How am I doing? Bit of spray-shot there, but some of it not far off the mark, I would guess.

Well, you could just pack up and leave, I suppose. Find yourself somewhere less claustrophobic, where nobody cares a damn about anybody else. Or, as you suggest, you could do something outrageous. Can't see you doing that, mind you, unless my Botticelli Venus has grown sharp nails since we last met.

Of course one thing that would fit the bill would be for you to go to bed with every man in the street – prove you're no coward, you can take it lying down! I've always thought it would be a witty idea to do something like that – rock the boat properly (or improperly) – make a bet with someone, perhaps. Let's see, what would the bet be? What could I offer that might be worth it? One of my debenture tickets for Wimbledon: how about that? Hardly for you in any case, you're far too nice – although you have of course made a start. Only eight to go.

But I'm being facetious. Honestly, I think you should do what I suggested: put yourself in a bit of an isolation ward for the winter, then come out here and let your hair down in the spring, and I guarantee I shall make you the belle of the ball.

Anyway, do please keep cheerful if you can, and make sure you have a good Christmas. Here the ambassador has vomit-making plans for making your Messiah wish he'd never been born. As a tainted Jewess I'm brushing up my Orthodox excuses from being included. Piers is contemplating a hasty conversion and is studying the Talmud.

Love in idleness,

Ruth.

LONDON W4 1000 HRS DECEMBER 17
CABLE DESPATCH TO: RUTH CONWAY
69 DAMASKINOU NEAPOLIS ATHENS
GREECE
BET TAKEN STOP SEE YOU ON CENTRE
COURT STOP LOVE JANICE

December 26th

Dear Piers,

As you see, I've become a 'Catcher in the Rye', with nothing to catch except Legionnaires Disease from the food.

You may well ask what I'm doing here; I've spent much of my Christmas asking the same question. The truth is, 'Recommended by the British Tourist Board, Christmas catered for.' They should have added, 'Husbands in the doghouse definitely not catered for.' So far it's been family orgies of Blue Nun and crackers, with cheek-to-cheek dancing between the baldies and the bouffons. I was designated a small table in the corner for Christmas dinner and commanded by the local Securitate to wear a paper hat. The slice of turkey was sun-dried, with gravy like an oil slick, but I got passably merry on a bottle of Morgon and several armagnacs, and retired to bed to the sound of someone vomiting next door. Today the silence of hangovers is deafening, and as I sit here under my friendly forty-watt ceiling light I'm roused by the thought that I'm only twenty-nine exciting miles from Eastbourne.

A pretty town though, Rye. A good place to die.

The reason I'm here is because J showed me the red card. I was obviously mistaken not to have taken my banishment seriously, because when I phoned from Heathrow she said she'd get the police if I turned up. Something in her voice told me to believe her. So I got the train into town and now here I am with a small hire-car, indigestion and a paper hat. Tomorrow, thank God, it's back to Bucharest the fun-city – and jolly New Year reports from the Aids hospital.

I've been trying to work out the issues in this messy business. I know I'm entirely to blame and all that, and of course I should never have lied to J about Amanda. All the same, to bar a man from his own house and family at Christmas is a bit steep, don't you think? I bet Ruth would never do that to you, and don't tell me you haven't deserved it. There's a steely virtue about Janice that refuses to take account of the way life's been these past twelve years. The truth is I've slogged my guts out earning a living, sweating it out in ghastly places without any home comforts. I've risked my neck in wars, interviewed terrorists, received death threats and contracted horrible diseases. And what has Janice done all that time? Gone 'goo-gi-goo' with her baby, flirted with the antiques business, painted three murals and played a great deal of tennis. Now she sits in the house I bought, while I pay the mortgage and pull crackers in Hotel Paradiso. All because I flirted with a few neighbours and then screwed one who dropped her knickers and begged for it. What's more, in six months' time, when Janice finally condescends to let me crawl back, I bet you the first thing she tells me – firmly and proudly – is that unlike me, she hasn't had anyone since I left. She'll wear her goodness like a suit of armour and it'll be like going to bed with Joan of Arc.

Sorry this is a sour letter, but I need to get things off my chest. Perhaps I should have followed my first instinct and stayed right away – gone somewhere that hadn't heard of Christmas. Sri Lanka, perhaps, or Marrakesh. Except that I suspect everyone takes Christmas with them and there's not a place where there aren't sleigh bells.

Besides, I felt a strange tug of the heart. I wanted to be in England, in the same country as J and C. I thought of Clive waking up to his stocking yesterday morning at some unheard-of hour, and I felt a real pang at not having been Father Christmas to put it there. And I thought of Janice alone, just as I was alone.

Regrets. Regrets. For what might have been. As it is, Amanda threatens to turn up in the New Year. I don't actually think that's what I want at all. Appetites sicken, and there's not too much in Bucharest to rekindle them. However, I hope the ambassadorial Xmas was as festive as here. Write to Bucharest if the spirit moves. After Rye I can assure you even Omsk would seem like Manhattan.

Yours in a paper hat,
Harry.

Dear Janice,

Who do you think you are – Circe?

If you're really serious, then I suppose I have to believe you; but this is definitely *not* the cool little blonde I know. Should I perhaps be heavy and aunt-like and warn you against . . . what? I'm not sure, because it does sound the most wicked and delicious idea – how clever of me to think of it! And yes, the bet is *on*, provided, a) I can trust you not to lie, and b) you give me a blow-by-blow-job account of each and every one of them. What is it? Eight to go! Also, no substitutes allowed, mark you; I'm not having you shying away from some beer-bellied scrap-merchant with halitosis just because you can make up the numbers with the Adonis who happens to be a weekend guest next door. We also have to agree on terms, i.e., French kissing under the mistletoe does *not* count, not even half a point; nor does a quick fumble behind the cocktail cabinet. I'm too refined a lady to spell out exactly what 'go to bed with' means, but I trust there's no scope for misunderstanding. I'm prepared to make one generous concession – I shall not insist on orgasms – they are too easily faked, and in any case one or two of your victims might find it beyond them.

So, you see I'm driving a hard bargain. Debenture seats at Wimbledon are not to be traded lightly, and I was not instructed by rabbis for nothing. *Shalom*! And *À l'attaque*! I shall await despatches from the front with eagerness.

To more solemn matters. Darling, how was Christmas? Did you manage to explain things to Clive, and was he terribly upset? I feel for you. It was brave to bar the door to Harry; you sounded distraught when you phoned, but you were absolutely right. The man's an uncaring bastard. And listen, why should you bother your pretty head about whether he ended up in a boarding-house for Christmas? A bawdy-house more likely – rummaging inside the Christmas stockings. Good riddance.

Our Christmas. Well, what would you like to know? Piers behaved quite immaculately at the ambassador's reception. I did not. Mrs Conway is not seen to be an asset to a diplomat's career, and in Piers's view I've now ensured that his first ambassadorial post will be some fundamentalist hell-hole where women are veiled and locked up at night. I've promised divorce proceedings in that event, which he agrees to on the grounds that he'll be allocated a harem in any case.

The rest of Christmas was calm. Piers gave me a superb fire-opal necklace made by some Greek craftsman he knows. Says it suits me, but it tickles my cleavage. I gave him a Folio Society edition of Herodotus which will keep him quiet. Yesterday, Boxing Day, we went to a little restaurant we like near the Tower of the Winds – my favourite part of Athens (in fact my only favourite part of Athens) – and Piers proved to me that there are Greek wines worth drinking. So, that should improve the quality of life in the First Secretary's garret without, I hope, improving my chances of a repeat invitation to the ambassadorial residence.

Now I must go. And you, my Circe, have work to do. The Irish are throwing a diplomats' hooley – heaven help us.

With love and crossed fingers,

Ruth.

January

My darling Clive,

Have you decided what you want your bedroom mural to be, I wonder? Sorry I had to say no to your first idea, but your mother isn't Michelangelo – not yet at least – and portraits of the entire Tottenham Hotspur football team in action at Wembley Stadium isn't really a subject I'd feel happy tackling. I had in mind something more countrified; you know, fields, animals, flowers and things, with perhaps Spindle stretched out in the sun. I'm quite good at drawing cats.

But of course if you have other ideas do let me know and I'll do my best to have it done for you by the Easter holidays. My mural for No 7 is pronounced a triumph, by the way. I'm trying to get out of doing one for No 4; he's our rather dour Scottish doctor, and I'm sure he's going to want some windswept loch with bagpipers and stags at bay, and I like doing things that are bright and cheerful, which he most certainly is not. I suspect he's taken a little bit of a shine to me, and I begin to wish I hadn't registered with his surgery.

The other piece of news is that No 8 – a very grand Royal Academician – wants to paint my portrait, he says. He sees me as Flora, goddess of flowers. I bet *you* don't – just bossy old Mum. Oh yes, and the rather shy historian at No 5 has decided I ought to go bird-watching with him. He gets terribly excited when some pterodactyl gets blown off course on to our local disused reservoir; he drags me off there to admire the bedraggled thing. 'No, not *that* one, that's a duck,' he says, turning my binoculars round the other way. But they all look the same to me, and Jesus, it's cold out there.

So you see I'm getting in with the neighbours. I realise I've never lived in a community since I was a schoolgirl, and then it was quite different because all we ever talked about was boyfriends. I remember Ruth – you know, the one who's now in Athens – saying very firmly that there were far too many boys in the world to settle for just one of them, and then straight out of school she went and married Piers, through whom of course I eventually met Daddy.

Having got to the subject of Daddy, I ought to say something more about his not having been with us at Christmas. I know how disappointing that was for you. The truth is, darling, Daddy and I have come to feel it might be best if we weren't together all the time. We're both terribly important to one another, and of course we both love you madly, but we've become very different people who need different things, and sometimes it can make for an easier relationship if you aren't too close.

In that way we can remain real friends without getting on each other's nerves. In time I hope you'll be able to understand this. It's hard, I know, and I hate to make you unhappy. But please believe me, it's for the best in the long run, and I promise you we'll work out how you can still see Daddy a lot. At the moment, as you know, he's in Romania, but he won't always be there. And as soon as he's back, we'll all work something out together.

Remember how enormously you matter to us both. It hasn't been easy to tell you all this, but I think you're old enough now to realise that living together isn't always simple, not even for mums and dads.

We'll have a lovely time at Easter. Would you like to ask your friend from Exmoor to stay?

I love you so much, so very much, darling.

Mummy.

Dearest Ruth,

I've just written a painfully difficult letter to Clive. Thought about it for hours and it still reads as though dictated by an agony aunt. Over Christmas I couldn't bring myself to spoil his fun by bringing up the subject of Harry and me; so I lived with the lie that it was work pressure. But now I've done it – as gently as I could. God, one feels such guilt. How we long to keep children wrapped in motherly blankets. The idyll of the perfect parent must be about the last enduring family myth – certainly more enduring than the idyll of the perfect marriage.

Talking of which – now I'm using my Circe voice – since I've been on my own again I've been reconnoitring the battleground, surveying targets and testing weak points in the defences. You're right: I'm absolutely not the cool little blonde you used to know. Harry killed her off. Now I'm a born-again predator. (Mind you, so was Venus: she wasn't Botticelli's cool little blonde either, was she?) Actually I feel more like a crusader than a predator. I've spent so many of my thirty-five years trying to be worthy of gentle Jesus meek and mild, and sod it, look where it got me – almost middle-aged before I had a good fuck. So from now on I'm going to fight the good fight. I know you'll laugh at me because you discovered this years ago, but my surprise romp with

Amanda's husband was an eye-opener (well, they were actually closed much of the time, but you know what I mean). For the first time in my life I gave in completely to sheer pleasure. There was no time to put up defences. The drawbridge was down, and so were my knickers. No holding back. No 'I must try and enjoy it', no hurrying to the bathroom for a clean-up and 'Phew, that's it for a few days'. I just loved it, loved it, all of it.

And I felt wonderful. Blessed. It was sex without any responsibilities – something I'd never had, and God am I going to make up for lost time! And if you think about it – says she, trying to justify herself after all – if I decide to make love to nine men, that's still only a fraction of the number of times Harry's been having it off these last umpteen years – probably a fraction of the times he's had it off with Ah-man-dah. So you see I'm actually being very moderate, almost ladylike, you might say. Positively chaste. In the mirror I look virginally pure.

Christ, it's ridiculous, Ruth. Harry's been assuming for years that his willy's got a manly right to go 'ping' every time he meets someone he fancies. That's what a willy's for, he would say. No guilt at all. Just a matter of if, how, when, where, and yippee! But me, oh no! If I fancied someone then I thought there was something wrong with me – married women aren't supposed to do that sort of thing – I'd betrayed myself – and those hot dreams in the night were visitations of the devil. Well, not quite the devil, but I certainly used to feel ashamed. What garbage! What a waste! Not any longer. I want it, and I want it good.

Another thing – I felt too shy to tell you in my last letter – Harry is rather small, I now realise. He doesn't actually – well, you know what I mean – I still feel shy. He doesn't reach. I wonder if this is why he's spent so much time getting it up with other women; perhaps he imagines that with continual use it'll stretch, the poor little fellow. It also makes me wonder why Ah-man-dah chooses to exchange an Aston Martin for a Morris Minor. Perhaps it's to do with fuel consumption. All the same I'm a little anxious in case I'm only experiencing the thin end of the wedge. If the laws of progression persist at this rate, I may have to call off the bet.

Progress so far, as I've said, is largely reconnaissance: beginning to establish undiplomatic relations. My Scottish doctor at No 4, Angus, is a promising early candidate. The fates have provided me with one of my perfectly harmless small lumps on the right breast, so that'll be a good starting point. A touch of perfume will help: Giorgio, I think. Then there's Roger the medieval historian at No 5 – the one with the lush of a wife. He's a bird-watcher, I discovered, so I've faked a passion for our feathered friends which has already landed me with several perishingly cold duck-watches with the aid of Harry's binoculars. Christ, birds are boring. Then there's Ambrose the RA at No 8 (with the wife who's a walking prayer-mat). He's keen to paint me as Flora for the Summer Exhibition. Flora in January! Spring flowers in April or May, he says deadly seriously. I've had a look round his studio and all his sitters look clothed for the North Pole. Not a nude in sight. Not even a whisper of a cleavage. So how will I suggest that mythologically Flora should surely wear only flowers? Ruth, can you really see me posing with a garland of daffodils and crocuses in my navel? Would that turn him on, or merely bring his wife in with the rolling-pin?

For the rest, no progress yet. Bill the architect is the one I want most in order to pay Nina back, and I think he'll be a pushover. He might enjoy breasts he can actually get his hands round. Courtenay the would-be Labour MP is likely to have plenty of time on his hands in the present political climate. His wife – when she's not breeding – is a lady novelist as heavy as her books and much the same shape. By the way, I'm going on the principle of looking at all their wives to see what men *don't* like, and determining to be the opposite. So I am very Tory and do *not* read lady novelists.

That leaves the advertising mogul at No 9, Maurice. Absolutely no problem there, judging by the bedroom eyes and the miserable wife Lottie. Then there's the soft-porn movie director Kevin, next door to me. The only difficulty there is going to be holding up the traffic in bimbos for long enough. I imagine he'll be dreadful – all aftershave and, 'Do you a favour darlin'' – but mercifully quick.

Now comes the real headache: 'Arold at No 3. Ruth, this may be a price too high even for a debenture ticket at Wimbledon. There is a ray of hope, however. 'Arold and Ivy are talking of selling. I'm thinking of offering my services to the estate agents, free. Then of course I could hand-pick the buyer, couldn't I? You wouldn't call that cheating, would you?

God, I'm exhausted just thinking about all this. On

a very sober note, though, I shall need to be very careful. A stock of condoms at all times, following your example, oh wise one. But I've never bought one before. Can I really bring myself to walk into the chemist and say, 'A dozen condoms, please'? Supposing they ask, 'What kind, madam?' Or even worse, 'What size, madam?' Do they come in different sizes, different colours? I don't know. I suppose I could always say coolly, 'One of each, please,' couldn't I? But that's only the beginning. When the occasion arises (so to speak) what does one do? You seemed to know with your Greek toyboy. Well, I certainly don't. Does one keep a sharp eye on the thing until it's all upstanding and then say, 'Hold it there a moment', quickly fumble in the handbag, select one that looks suitable and sort of ram it on? Or do I hand it to him like a bunch of flowers, 'I brought this specially for you, darling, I do hope it's the kind you like'? And all the time I'll be lying there stretched out waiting for the great gift of manhood; hardly the posture for this sort of *badinage*, is it? And what do I do if it falls off in the middle, or bursts?

Please, please advise.

I tell you, it's no simple matter preparing to lay the street. And if Wimbledon is rained off after all this, I'll shoot myself.

Enough of my worries. The weather's turned bitter, with wandering flakes of snow. I hope all these houses have central heating.

Love,

Janice.

Somewhere unpronounceable
in central Greece

January 10th (I think)

Dear Janice,

This began life as a postcard but I could see it was going to spill over. Bright cold weather in Athens, so Piers and I have taken off for a weekend's skiing. I've no idea where we are or how the hell we got here in the VW. Piers is almost as dangerous behind the wheel as he is on skis. He applies the same rules – slides into everything while practising his Greek over his right shoulder, in this case to a shellshocked government minister who volunteered to show us this place. Plus wife who looks like Melina Mercouri (perhaps *is* Melina Mercouri).

Anyway, we have the minister's chalet and a roaring fire. The skiing is hazardous; the ski-hoists operate on the principle that what goes up must come down, usually with me on them. I am bruised but undaunted. The minister is an anglophile and claims to love cricket: he has to be a fraud. I've tried to probe him about the Cretan Bank scandal but he's effusively reticent (if you can imagine what I mean) and I suspect bought his ski chalet and no doubt a yacht or two out of the proceedings.

The après-ski is dreadful, full of Athenian yuppies as sleek as salamanders. At least they don't do Zorba's dance or smash plates. Melina Thing knocks back Johnny Walker Black Label like a rhino at a water-hole. The minister's concession to Pasok Socialism is to stick to retsina, and when he's consumed enough of it he waxes lyrical about his peasant origins on the island of Kythira. Does that name ring a bell? Birthplace of Aphrodite, remember? I didn't know the place really existed. But he swears it's beautiful and unspoilt and I should go there in the spring. Naturally he has a house there, too. So, I might. Why don't you come too? Take time off from your conquests and join me. What could be more apt than the birthplace of Aphrodite? Janice stepping naked out of the foam. I'm serious; do think about it.

Tomorrow it's back to Athens. The ambassador's invited us to dinner, horror of horrors. I imagined I'd be spared such things after my Christmas performance (apparently I told the Austrian cultural attaché to fuck off – can't remember why). Piers is behaving like Professor Higgins and instructing me how to behave 'proper'.

Lots of love, and how's the score?

Ruth.

PS A story currently doing the rounds of the embassy is that the American ambassador claims to possess a Teflon erection: hard, long-lasting, non-stick. Even Piers is quite shocked.

Dear Piers,

I have a new *pied-à-terre*. Actually, a *pied-sous-terre*, the 'a' part of the address referring to the basement. I am buried here temporarily, having been summoned back from Bucharest awaiting an even jollier assignment: Vilnius. Lithuania in mid-winter – what fun! The boss thinks I should be delighted since I'm now to be referred to as, 'Our Eastern Europe Correspondent'. He points out, rightly of course, that seldom has a single arena of the world (he talks like that) undergone such dramatic changes, and any reporter should be privileged to witness them. Have you noticed how often men with highly-paid sinecures refer to those who do the dirty work as 'privileged'? We had lunch at the Caprice, and he mentioned a five-grand pay rise, which will come in useful now that I'm paying for this rabbit-hole as well as supporting madam in the family manse.

No further communication from that direction, except for a sweet drawing from Clive of the new kitten which he made look like a tiger with toothache. Bless him. He's the one I miss most. I don't even know what J has told him. The drawing just said, 'With love from Clive,' which broke me up.

Your account of the embassy Christmas cheered me greatly. Did Ruth really do that? Mind you, the

Austrian probably *was* a Nazi just like his president, but I always thought embassy wives weren't supposed to go round telling the truth. That's meant to be my job. What intrigues me is how well I tell the truth to a camera and how badly I do it to Janice. Quite different things, I know, yet one becomes easily self-deluded in this job, assuming after a while that anything one utters must be true. In your job I suppose you must have quite the opposite experience.

The luscious Amanda was here for the weekend, leaving the long-suffering Robert in charge. She says he's always been a hopeless lover and now can't even get it up. What bleak horizons so many marriages have, mine included; the grindstone that should sharpen passions merely blunts them. What I miss are the little things passion doesn't touch – listening to music together, going for walks, the wave from the window, laughter, planning holidays, the smell of toast while I'm shaving. And of course Clive. Perhaps kids are really the best reason for marriage – though there *you* are, you have an enviable marriage and no kids at all. Maybe I've just got it wrong, and must settle for what I am. What I am at the moment is Gorby's watchdog in the Baltics. How faith in the man has collapsed. No tyrant is more dangerous than a benevolent one, because we all want to love him, and that love blinds us to the terrible things he does. I, meanwhile, have acquired a Russian fur hat with ear-flaps (hear no evil, speak no evil). It appears that journalists' lady-friends are not allowed in Lithuania, which will be good for my sperm-count. Amanda is miserable, I less so.

Best wishes from the underworld,

Yours,

Harry.

1 River Mews

January 18th

My darling Clive,

It was so lovely to get your letter. You know, what you said about Daddy and me was so adult; I was really proud of you. Of course we'll both of us always love you. And if, as you say, you feel relieved to be like everyone else at school at last, then that's even better, isn't it? You ask about divorce: well, it isn't quite as quick and simple as all that, whatever your friend may say. Nor does it actually mean you'll have two mummies and two daddies to give you birthday presents. At least not at the moment. If I should happen to meet someone I like then of course I would tell you straightaway, and I'm sure Daddy would do the same. But that's all rushing it a bit. And I don't think that just because your Mr Watson is single and has a Jaguar he would necessarily want to marry me, however nice you've told him I am. Maybe I wouldn't like him, anyway. Who knows?

No news here. Snow is still lying about, going grey and slushy. I had to visit the doctor this week; nothing at all serious but he had to examine me rather carefully and he had very cold hands.

I'll write again very soon. Take care and I hope you score some more goals.

Lots and lots of love,

Mummy.

1 River Mews

January 18th

Dearest Ruth,

I'm in a philosophical mood; bear with me. I'm realising how making love opens a cupboard door in people's lives, and sad and terrible things come tumbling out. Why had I always imagined it was just about sex?

But first let me tell you about the hypocritic oath. The lump was duly reported to Dr A this week, and since he lives three doors down there was no problem agreeing on a home visit rather than a trek to the NHS surgery. I suggested 'after hours' and 'stay and have a drink'; I thought that might break down a few barriers. But Angus still came to the door bristling with efficiency: doctor's briefcase, professional voice, a rationed smile, 'Now, let's have a look.' I heard myself being fey and awkward, which was absurd, of course; the man sees boobs of all shapes and sizes every day of the year – probably finds them no more arousing than ingrowing toenails. And he examined me so quickly, with a grunt of, 'Nothing to worry about there,' that I was almost panicky over what to do next. I thought he'd say 'No thanks' to the drink and 'Cheerio'. Collapse of seduction. Bet lost.

I suppose I broke the rules by handing him a glass of wine still half-dressed; it wasn't deliberate, I was so flustered I didn't think twice about it. A minute or two earlier it had been all clinical – doctor-patient – no-nonsense. Suddenly it was erotic to be holding out a glass to him with my breasts bare. I could feel it cut through his professional guard, and he tried not to look at me as he took it. 'You're on your own, I gather,' he said. I wondered who had told him. Then he tried to distance himself again with a bit of bluff. 'Not for long, a beautiful woman like you.' And he laughed. He sounded like Nina for a moment.

'Do you think so?', I asked. It was the only bit of flirting I did. He didn't answer. The longer I stood there the more naked I felt, and the more he tried not to look at me. His awkwardness made him strangely attractive: strong, craggy face, badly shaved. 'I always have done,' he said eventually, making a point of coughing as if to cover up what he'd said. I thought of his doctor-wife, hair in a bun, sensible clothes, striding to work. Then I caught his eye. He looked helpless suddenly, and gave another little cough. 'We're off-duty, that's understood, isn't it?' And that was that. I took the rest of my clothes off.

He wasn't a particularly good lover, but it didn't matter. It was good for me. The curious thing, Ruth, was that I kept thinking of the first time I went to bed with Harry, and how incredibly different it was. I'd fancied him so much, yet when it came to it I remember feeling sick with nerves. I kept resisting, holding on to my clothes, trying not to look. In the end, Harry virtually raped me. I've never had the courage to tell you before, but I never had an orgasm with Harry. Never. I used to give myself one in the bathroom afterwards. And yet I loved him, I really loved him. We had a good life, and it would have been enough for me. 'Would it?', I can hear you say. 'Look at you now.' Maybe. Well, I've certainly learnt to laugh. Perhaps they go together, laughter and sex.

After we'd made love I lay on the bed with Angus drinking some more wine, and he started telling me about his wife – Christ, I'm beginning to realise they all do – and how sex didn't really matter between them, never had, there was no time, being a doctor was the thing, and they both saw bodies all day and every day. Then he began to get dressed rather hurriedly. 'We're never going to do this again,' he said, 'I might fall in love with you.' 'Bad for the practice?', I suggested a bit cattily, just lying there all naked. He didn't know what to say, and went on dressing very neatly. 'I'm not into falling in love,' I said. 'I just like sex when I feel like it.'

Ruth, *I* said that, not you! Good little me. The girl Harry always called frigid, who never wore a *décolleté*, always undressed in the bathroom, never flirted for fear of turning men on and not being able to cope. Janice, the nice wife who gave dinner parties, didn't drink and had headaches. Janice, who used to hope Harry would come to bed too pissed to do anything.

'Let's forget about this evening,' Angus said at the door as he was leaving; he was the visiting doctor again. 'It was nice,' I answered. 'I don't need to forget it. I'm a woman on my own, remember, Doctor. I can do what I like.' He just nodded, and I think he felt angry. Perhaps more with himself than with me. He'd told me more than he wanted to, and now he had to go back to his cage.

And what do I feel? Puzzled, really. The thing is, for years I've watched men parade their sexuality, looking for plunder, wanting one thing only. It was women who were always supposed to want more than that, and had to say no for fear of being hurt, diminished, reduced in some way, or whatever. But it isn't like that. Now it's *me* who only wants one thing, and look what happens: it's men who turn out to want everything else as well – a shoulder to weep on, a confessor, a nanny, a guardian angel. Christ, Ruth, I could set up in practice: 'Janice Blakemore, Rent-a-Cuntsellor'.

Except it's me who's learning so much. It's an education.

Meanwhile, I have to tell you my angelic son is a scheming little beast. The agonies I went through searching for just the right words to tell him about Harry and me, and do you know what? He's known all along – was surprised we'd got together again – thank heaven it's out in the open at last, he said, and now he can compare notes with his friends. The boy is not even twelve! I found some magazines in his cupboard the other day I didn't even know existed, let alone you could buy.

My sweet little boy! Do you know, he's even told some French master at school who's single that I'd make him a good wife. The humiliation of it. Where did innocence go? Be thou as a little child. Not this one: the boy's a monster.

The skiing sounded fun. I think the Teflon erection is quite disgusting. Can you send me one? As for Kythira, it sounds like a wonderful idea, but cash is a problem. I feel guilty being kept in sin by a banished husband when I'm earning about ten pence a month flogging junk jewellery. Also, April's no month for Aphrodite to be rising from the foam. Could we put the idea on hold for the time being?

More anon. Two down: seven to go.

With love,

Janice.

January 22nd

Dear Janice,

However unwelcome, I wanted to get in touch, at least to tell you where I am. The atmosphere here is tense in the extreme, as you can imagine. A city of Davids waiting for Goliath in the snow.

I'm now, by the way, Eastern Europe Correspondent, which means I'm liable to be pushed around the place even more. Typical media pettiness – apparently the Moscow correspondent is indignant that I'm here, not him, on the grounds that Lithuania is still officially part of the Soviet Union. That's Eamonn, whom you've met a few times: nasty little Kremlin creep.

It's pretty lonely here; very few journalists. Even fewer facilities. My fortieth birthday next week and I'm wondering where all the years went. The best of them were with you, do you know that? I miss you, and I miss our life. I think of you alone in London and me alone here, and it seems such a waste – such a mess I've made of it. I like to believe I can still put it right, if you'll let me try again.

Meanwhile, I have a fat pay rise. Do you have enough, what with school fees, etc? I'd be happy to increase it.

I hold a picture of you in my mind, my beautiful girl. You were always the only one who counted.

With love,

Harry.

Dear Piers,

Very briefly, here is my new igloo; might just as well be underground, even the daylight is rationed here. There are compensations: only a trickle of press corps, but it includes a buxom tart from the *Washington Post* whose understanding of *glasnost* may not be quite what Mr Gorbachev had in mind. Father is said to own half the state of Iowa. Certainly the girl looks corn-fed.

This turns out to be one of those news hot-spots where there's no news at all. Like the best classical drama the action is all off-stage. Doesn't make it easy to fix the camera with an urgent stare.

For God's sake, find me a Greek story. Something I can get my teeth into.

Yours in limbo,

Harry.

LONDON W4 1200 HRS JANUARY 25
CABLE DESPATCH TO: BLAKEMORE
BALTIC HOTEL VILNIUS LITHUANIA
HAPPY BIRTHDAY NO THANKS STOP
JANICE

69 Damaskinou
Neapolis
Athens

January 25th

Dear Janice,

If that's your idea of a philosophical letter then what may I expect on your return to earth? I've been thinking how curious it is, this business of exchanging letters – quaint in the age of word processors, fax machines, phones and telexes. If we were both of us in London we'd never write at all; yet it strikes me – and now I'm catching your thoughtful mood – that one says things in letters which would never be said face to face. Why? Is distance a safety curtain? Is it because we have time to think? Or does the laborious business of putting pen to paper induce a most terrible honesty?

When Piers was in the Yemen as a junior and it was considered unwise for a Jewish wife to join him, we used to write regularly and I got to know him far better than I believe I do now. In fact I look at him sometimes shovelling his boring old papers into a briefcase to go to the embassy, and I say to myself, 'Who is this man?' Today it was even worse. I arranged to meet him for lunch. I walked into the restaurant, saw no one I recognised, and sat down. It must have been a full ten minutes before a man who'd been sitting three tables away came over and said, 'Are you waiting for someone, Mrs Conway?' Needless to say it was Piers. Do you suppose what happens is that we get an imprint of a person at a certain moment of their life – like a photo on a dressing-table – and simply fail to notice that the person has changed? Like *The Picture of Dorian Gray* in reverse.

Well, that's my intellectual contribution for the year; don't expect anything but scandal from now on. Do you think we both of us actually suffer from a chronic lack of education? I'm convinced that I understand absolutely nothing of what goes on in the world outside my own preoccupations, and that it's all Piers's fault for plucking me straight from school when he – the bastard – had already honed his mind on three years at Cambridge. And you, you're no better off: I know you went to that weird art school, but what did that teach you other than how to look gorgeous, marry a complete prat, and become unemployable for the rest of your life?

There is of course another way of looking at it, which is that we're both of us lucky survivors of education, and never having been taught anything worthwhile, are free to be ourselves in a perfectly disgraceful way that would otherwise have been beaten out of us. Witness my entirely uncivilised lifestyle – about which more later – and your shocking treatment of the male libido in River Mews. Will you buy that version?

I don't like the sound of your doctor and I'm glad you got him out of the way early on. The bird-watching medieval historian sounds entirely sweet; my fear is that it's often capons who walk those medieval paths, hence the alcoholic wife who has it off with the milkman or whoever, and you may have to equip yourself with devices more persuasive than your big blue eyes to raise a twitch from your twitcher. (You could always start with a rousing chorus of, 'For he's a jolly good fellatio'.)

As for the portrait painter with the loony wife, you really shouldn't have too much trouble there, you know. Anyone who asks to paint you as Flora, my darling, is not a man who's sold his soul to boardroom portraiture and water-colours of the royal corgis. Just remind him you used to be an art student, and it'll reawaken all those tingling moments in the Sixties when he used to lean over eighteen-year-olds pretending to correct their drawings.

Don't know about the others. The failed Labour MP doesn't sound too much of a problem. All politicians have turgid sex lives if the Greek government's anything to go by, and being a failed politician will have made him as starved of adultery as he is of power. Look at all those kids; the poor man's had no alternative but to give it to his wife.

Sorry about 'Arold, but I'm not prepared to bend the rules just because you happen not to fancy a beer belly and poisonous breath. There are some sacrifices a girl has to make in this life, as I'm sure your mother told you. Mind you, twelve years with Harry might be said to be a sacrifice already beyond the call of duty. Poor Harry, you're making me feel quite sorry for him; I've half a mind to send him some powdered rhino's horn to make his willy grow. There's quite an illicit trade in the stuff in Athens, by the way. The Egyptians ship it into Piraeus and flog it to the Arab terrorists, who as you know live here in alarming quantities, many of them next to our beloved ambassador.

Which brings me to the ambassadorial dinner last week. Piers had done sterling work as Professor Higgins and I was decorum itself – very stylish, darling. Full-length black dress, not a hint of cleavage, little black purse (condom removed), hair swept up into a French pleat, pearl choker à la Princess Di, tasteful perfume, smile fixed to perfection, topics of conversation all prepared as delicately as the canapés. You would have been proud of me. After cocktails I was placed next to the French ambassador, which I could see from the look on Piers's face was no small honour, and from the looks on the other ladies' faces was the cause of no small resentment.

Anyway, he was lovely. Perfect English, of course. Voice like vintage champagne. Handsome enough to die for. Designer-grey hair above the ears. How do the French produce these paragons? I was made to feel witty and uniquely marvellous, as though he'd been waiting to meet me all his life. That is *real* charm. By the end of the main course I had a strong urge to place my hand on his crutch and say in my most vigorous French, so my neighbours wouldn't understand: '*Ecoute, beau monsieur l'ambassadeur, je suis tout à fait mouillée à cause de toi. Si tu desire une maîtresse anglaise très sexy, je suis entièrement prête. En attendant le pudding nous pouvons disparaître dans la salle de bain et faire l'amour magnifique sous le portrait de la reine Elizabeth par Annigoni. J'aimerais beaucoup ça.*' Well, I didn't, did I? We got a little merry instead, and when he discovered I was lapsed-Jewish he laughed and came out with several very sophisticated Jewish jokes which were also very funny. Then he claimed it was invariably Jews who told the best Jewish jokes, and didn't I know any? So, as a diversion for my lust I told him one of my favourites – you know, the one about the rabbi, the pork and the prostitute. I told it rather well, I thought (there's nothing like feeling randy to make you articulate). What I didn't appreciate was that I also told it rather loudly, and that all conversation at the dinner table had ceased. I delivered the punch-line to a packed house.

I thought Piers would die. The ambassador's wife announced stridently that coffee was being served if we cared to retire to the drawing-room. I retired to the bathroom and wanted to slit my throat. The evening didn't survive too long, and Piers drove me home in radioactive silence. 'I'll be lucky to get the Pitcairn Islands after that,' he said as he closed the door of the flat. Then, thank God, he laughed.

Even by my standards it was truly awful. Do you think I could arrange for Piers to have a *maîtresse en titre* for these occasions in future?

And the French ambassador was so gorgeous. I never even said goodbye to him.

I feel quite miserable. How can I get out of this dreadful place ?

Yours in disgrace, but with much love,

Ruth.

Feburary

1 *River Mews*

February 5th

My darling Clive,

Have you had the same blizzard, I wonder? It's amazing here. At least a foot of snow. The car's a white bump, like a sheep with ears sticking out. Spindle adores it. I peer out of my bedroom window in the morning and her trails on the lawn look as though an army of snakes has been doing a training exercise. Then she comes belting in through the cat-flap and demands her Whiskas so urgently I have to hurry down not even dressed. We still don't have any curtains downstairs so I hope and pray nobody sees me.

I also hope *you* have the right clothes for the Arctic. Sadly, I imagine it's the end of football for the time being, isn't it? What do they make you do instead? In your last letter you talked about boxing. Do you really enjoy that – giving out black eyes and nose-bleeds? I dare say the boy you mention is a weed and a swot, but does that mean you have to disfigure him, too? I'd be much happier if you took up something like chess.

The main news here is that – amazingly – I have a rush of commissions for murals to paint. The doctor's one fell through – he doesn't seem to think his wife would appreciate what I do, and maybe he's right. But Bill the architect is so delighted with the house-boat one I did for his study that he wants another. He's also building some terribly grand flats on the river-front in Chelsea, and says two of the clients (Occidental Oil, I think) are keen to have me decorate their dining-rooms. I'm not hot on oil-rigs, but Bill's sure they have romantic visions of England and would much prefer Shakespeare country with swans, Ann Hathaway's cottage and stuff. Would you believe it, he's even prepared to pay my expenses to go off for a weekend and do some sketching around Stratford-upon-Avon in the spring?

And that's not all. Our immediate next door neighbour wants one too. He's Kevin – makes feature films, frightfully rich – you met him briefly over Christmas at that party. He showed me round the house the other day, and I must say he already has some very freaky pictures on the walls – by some Munich painter at the turn of the century called (would you believe it?) Baron von Stuck. All extremely valuable, he assures me. Kevin wants something more contemporary, he says; he showed me a spare room, apologising for the mess, with a blank wall opposite the window. Would I come up with some ideas, he asked me? Anyway, he's prepared to pay me lots of money.

The exciting thing, my darling, is that it means we may have some spare cash, so if you decide you do want to go skiing with the school party at Easter, I could probably afford it. Let me know.

Keep warm and safe. I'm glad to hear your French master wasn't too disappointed when you told him I wasn't thinking of getting married again just yet.

All my love,

Mummy.

1 River Mews

February 8th

Dearest Ruth,

Here beginneth, 'A Life in the Day of Janice Blakemore'. In short, yesterday (well, actually it began the day before).

First, Harry. A letter arrived from Vilnius – all firm-jawed contrition, thanks for the memory, plus the offer of a fat payrise as an incentive to re-open negotiations. Or maybe he was just strutting his stuff, playing the peacock for sweet little pea-hen who always takes him back in the end. Harry Blakemore, Our Eastern Europe Correspondent. Too bloody respondent by half, in my view.

I fired off a 'Thanks, no thanks' telemessage. When I put down the phone afterwards I was miserable. Why? I suppose because I used to love him such a lot. I ache for the loss of that. And for the little things, the little habits: 'When Harry gets back we'll . . .', 'I must remember to tell Harry.' Oh Ruth, he's forty soon, and I had such plans. Do you remember your mother, not long before our wedding? 'Are you quite sure, Janice? Pisces and Virgo. Tricky, my dear. Tricky.'

That evening, to cheer myself up, I went to bed with the new PD James. I put on my Janet Reger nightdress. Harry used to call it my seventh veil. I was quite shy wearing it, but now so what? I was on my own. Since when did women have to dress just for men? Which is how I happened to be wearing next to nothing for Maurice yesterday morning.

It was a day that began quietly. I drew back the bedroom curtains and peered out at the snow. The first sun for a week was streaking it pink and purple, and I wanted to paint it. Then came the clatter of the cat-flap and a horrendous yowling from Spindle demanding breakfast. As always I was too soft-hearted to tell her to bloody well wait, and took myself downstairs in my seventh veil, conscious that the only part that isn't see-through is the Janet Reger label. I hurried past the windows just in case, and thank God the house was warm because I'd forgotten to turn the heating down the night before. Anyway, I fed the cat who practically took the food straight out of the tin. Then I went to the front door to get the morning paper which was sticking out of the letter-box. As I pulled it out an envelope followed and plopped at my feet. Without thinking I opened the door: who on earth could be delivering me a note at 8 o'clock in the morning? And there, looking startled, was Maurice from No 9 – the ad-man – all spruced up and obviously on his way to the office. I could see his Jag parked outside just in front of my little Renault.

I said that Maurice looked startled, as well he might. He was just dropping in a party invitation from his wife, as it turned out. Instead, there was suddenly this blonde at the door, apparently posing as Salome.

Now, a good girl would have looked flustered, tried to cover herself up with an, 'Oh, terribly sorry', and hidden behind the door. This girl didn't; or rather she hesitated for that fatal split-second which is all that a professional hunter like Maurice needs. A smooth operator, that man; it was fascinating to see him at work. He smiled and said, 'This wouldn't be a place I could get a cup of coffee, I suppose, would it? It's been a long walk.' So I laughed and said, 'If you're in great need.'

My dear Ruth, this was 8 o'clock in the morning. I really do wonder about myself – though at that moment I found myself wondering about him. Legend has it that inside those Armani trousers is the most peripatetic plonker in London. (Harry shrivels by comparison.) The man wears his prowess like battle-honours. And he's pretty. Oh yes, you can just imagine the fluffy little heads turn as he strolls through the typing pool, and how he loves it. So here he was, on his way to the office, briefcase in hand, car keys jangling, client meeting no doubt at 9 o'clock, little wifey kissed goodbye two minutes ago at No 9, stepping into No 1 for a swift recce.

And here I was with a smile and practically nothing on. He was in luck. He suddenly found he had half an hour to spare. Don't miss a chance like this. A blonde for breakfast. Sets a man up for the day.

So I took his briefcase, led the way into the kitchen,

put on fresh coffee and sat demurely at the breakfast bar. He didn't waste a minute – busy executive and all that. Started playing the scene like the young Anthony Steele – fingers pushed through hair for that tousled, adorably confused look. Then the B-Movie lines began to roll out: 'You know, I haven't felt like this since I was sixteen . . . can you feel it too? Something between us . . .' Followed by the sudden intense look, a strong man stirred to the very depths. (Melt, girl, melt.) It was somewhat ruined, I have to say, by the percolator burp-burp-burping; none the less, that got me off the stool to pour the coffee, which gave him a chance to put his arm round me. 'Are you always this lovely in the morning?' 'No!', I said. He laughed. But I knew I shouldn't have said that because the laugh was a shade nervous. This woman doesn't know her lines; a bit too Bette Davis, not enough blonde *ingenue*.

What I should have done of course was a lot of, 'Oh Maurice, I don't know. Oh, we really mustn't,' and so on, while he came at me like a Stalin salute until I gradually melted into contented sighs. And the deed done, he would have departed with a smile and a glance at his Gucci watch, a pat on the cheek and, 'See you soon, sweetheart, thanks for the coffee.' Instead of which I leaned over and ran my fingers across his *membrum virile*, and said sweetly, 'Upstairs, don't you think?' You'd have thought I'd kicked him in his rising passion: instant detumescence, firm mouth in soft focus, eyes bulging. A cod-fish in a Turnbull and Asser shirt.

If the debenture seats hadn't depended on his coming up to scratch (ooops!) I'd have whisked myself out of the room there and then. And what an exit – Bette Davis to the life. As it was, I took his hand, led him up to the bedroom, and he followed like a lamb to the slaughter.

I'm sure that's exactly how he felt – used, exploited, gobbled up. All his terrors of the voracious vagina had come to haunt him one fine Wednesday morning in a des res in his own back yard. He undressed as though he was about to have a terminal operation, poor bastard. And I have to say, I loved it! As he wilted, I bloomed. 'It's never happened before, never,' he kept saying, gazing down angrily at his dangling thing. 'Never mind,' I said. 'Just relax. It's very pretty like that,' I added, lying. It looked like a Walls sausage half-skinned. Ruth, there is absolutely nothing erotic about a limp cock, is there? I kept being reminded of holding Clive's willy when I was teaching him to use the grown-up loo. Eventually, after mega-efforts on my part, things began to stir quite promisingly until the bloody cat leapt on to the bed and he went down again like a punctured tyre. Oh, ye gods! It took another half an hour, and all the time I was thinking, the man's missed his meeting and probably lost the Oxo account. Well, we made it finally; you'd have thought the walls of Jericho had fallen. 'Was it good for you?', he asked hopefully once he'd recovered his breath. 'Oh, wonderful,' I said. Actually, what I felt wonderful about was making him feel what he must have made so many women feel – that he was simply the means to a good wank. Harry used to make me feel that, too. Well, wifey strikes back. The sins of the husband visited upon the heads of the neighbours.

He went off like a schoolboy who's just been caned. I heard the Jag roar up the street. Then I suddenly thought of Myrna. Do you remember her at school? We used to stand guard outside the 'Girls' while she let the boys look up her skirt. A penny with knickers, sixpence without. Then she went and married whatsisname – that ginger-haired merchant banker (certainly no merchant bonker). And immediately the scarlet nail-varnish went: 'He says it looks like blood.' After that went the long nails: 'Talons'. No more bangles half-way up both arms: 'Too vulgar'. No more neckline half-way down the cleavage: 'Provocative'. And that look she got when she became too loud at parties. He ironed her out, remember, and promptly left her because she wasn't the woman he married.

After Maurice had gone I lay in the bath for ages. Hydrotherapy. Then I looked in the mirror at the sweet, petite blonde with the soft blue eyes whose husband had done her wrong, and I thought, you're exactly what the likes of Maurice would call a 'ball-breaking bitch'.

Oh Ruth, who would have thought castration could be so easy?

And so – pm – post-meridien, post-Maurice, post-meathead. Are you ready for the second chapter of my day?

I spent the afternoon preparing some drawings. This is where I have to tell you that I suddenly have *work* – lots of it. (Makes me realise how right old Brown Owl was at school, batting on about women needing creative work if they're going to be fulfilled. God, how we pitied and despised those old ducks snipping and daubing away as a channel for frustrated sexual energies. Well, I was Brown Owl yesterday.) The commissions are from Bill the architect, bloody Nina's husband (about which more anon). And one from none other than Kevin, the film director with the taste for bimbos. He turns out to be very sweet, a womaniser like you wouldn't believe, but courteous in a crude sort of way, East End lad made good and all that. Probably absolute hell to work for: directs from the casting-couch, etc. His films are a rape a minute, rather like his life at No 2. God, the sheer energy of the man.

It was about drinks time when the phone went, and it was him. 'Allo sweetheart,' all that stuff. 'Done any drawings for me yet?' Well, I had that afternoon. 'Bring 'em round then, if you're free.' 'Okay,' I said. What I'd actually done for Kevin – it's for a wall in a bedroom clearly used rather often – was clever, I thought. He hadn't known what he wanted – 'You're the fuckin' artist; I just make films and money' – so I'd roughed out a panorama, as if you were looking from a high window with a balcony and a river winding far away. Genuine Van Eyck stuff (perhaps I should have put a madonna praying in the foreground, topless. He might have liked that). Anyway, I thought it might appeal to a film director's longing to be lord of all he surveys.

So, that's what I took round. It was only a sketch, but a large one. Having looked me up and down – checking the contours – and mixed us both lethal martinis, he carefully unrolled the drawing across the kitchen table and weighted the corners with salt and pepper pots. It was an uneasy few moments, I can tell you. They seemed like an hour. Kevin said nothing, just grunted occasionally. His hair, dramatically grey, kept flopping over his face as his eyes followed the meandering of the river, and every so often he'd peer through the curtain of hair and the eyes would meander over me.

Eventually he stood back and said, 'Fuckin' marvellous. Clever little lady, aren't you? Real art, that is.' I made some inane remark like, 'Oh, do you really think so?' 'Of course I fuckin' do,' he bellowed. 'I don't waste bloody compliments. Ask the girls who come 'ere. Researchers.' And he gave a laugh. 'You've seen 'em. I tell 'em, if their brains were 'alf as large as their tits they'd be fuckin' Einstein. You're the other way round: large brain, small tits.' He laughed again. Then suddenly he said, 'Seen any of my films, 'ave you?' I was honest. 'One.' 'What ya reckon, then?' I don't know if it was his remark about tits and brains, or the gin, but my mouth opened and I heard myself spill out a bit of a tirade. 'Crude and violent, frankly,' I said. 'Not a scrap of wit or characterisation. Women just bits of property being banged by perverts. The dong as a weapon. Stupid, infantile men's games.' And to my astonishment, I burst into tears.

Poor Kevin. He came rushing out from behind the table, great chunks of hands flailing helplessly, not knowing whether to pat me or slap me. Tears were pouring down my face into the martini, and I could feel my nose beginning to drip. I managed to say, 'Handkerchief', and he dived into his pocket and produced a huge square of white silk. I snuffled into it for a few moments while he topped up the martinis. Then he asked, 'What about yer 'usband, then? Where's 'e gone?' I managed to nod and splutter that we'd separated. ''Avin it orf, was 'e? Stoopid bugger. Girl like you, fuckin' stoopid.'

I felt grateful to him for saying that, and the flood of tears began to dry up. Then I said, feeling all brave and righteous, 'But you do it too. Why? Why do men need to have all these women? Tell me. Look at the parade of bimbos through here – all tits and bums and legs that go right up to their G-spots.' He seemed surprised, as if he'd never given it a thought before. 'Dunno really.' Then he suddenly looked interested. 'Maybe it's the last great adventure,' he said. 'You know, my great-grandad worked on a ship. Ended up in India. Loved it, 'e did – colonising the place, I suppose you'd say. I still read the letters 'e wrote. 'E said it was a heathen land, and 'e was there when they raised the flag above its highest mountain. 'Ow about that? A whole fuckin' continent. Well, I can't do that, can I? The only thing I'm goin' to raise my flag over is a woman.'

'I see,' I said. 'Just another cunt-ry?' And he laughed, a great bellow of a laugh that bounced off the walls. We both laughed. ''Ere, Janice. You're all right, you really are.' And he gave me a hearty slap on the back.

I could see he was troubled at the same time. He didn't actually like what I'd said at all. It seemed to bother him. He sat down hard with his legs round the back of the chair facing me, looking challenging. 'Let me tell you something, girl. Before you gives me and every other bloke stick, you oughta think about the women. Me and 'Arry out there aren't exactly rapin' 'em, y'know. We're not talking innocent victim of male lust (he did a brilliant imitation of Ah-man-dah's loud, prissy voice). The bimbos have a good time. They don't 'ave to come 'ere. It's not, "Strip off or yer fired". Not white slave traffic. It's their bloody adventure too; they want a good fuck from someone they think's famous. Well, I'm famous for that, anyway. They know that.' And he gave another of those bellowing laughs. 'As for Mandy down the road – she hasn't got a sell-by date stamped on 'er bum, y'know. She's sittin' up there on the fuckin' shelf floggin' 'erself to anyone who'll purchase. I bought it once and very nice too. Juicy. I mean, what's a bloke supposed to do? Tie a knot in it? Anyway, what've you been doin' since you found old 'Arry screwing some other bloke's wife? Weepin' into yer pillow, 'ave you?'

I don't know what came over me – perhaps it was hearing that he'd had Amanda – but I said, 'No, screwing everyone else's husband.'

And now I know what 'gobsmacked' means. His face went white, his mouth dropped open, and I could see a little muscle begin to jump about on his cheek. Then, very softly, he said, 'Well, fuck me sideways. You beauty, you.' He gazed at me for a long while, and everything began to change.

Do you want to hear the rest? Well, we went upstairs and he started to undress me, and I swear it was as though I was the most precious thing he'd ever handled. He was unbelievably tender. It was like silk touching me with those huge hands. He had the body of an ape, but it didn't matter. He made love as if he was Byron, and it blew my mind.

God knows what hour it was when I left. He made me an omelette – I couldn't help noticing the same easy skill with his hands. As he helped me on with my coat he stroked my hair and said, 'Yeah, you are lovely. I could love you easy. Someone ought to.' Then he rather spoilt it by adding, 'And 'ow much yer gonna fleece me for the paintin', or *mooral* as you call it?' I laughed and said I wouldn't name a sum now or it might seem like 'for services rendered'. 'Extra-mural activities,' I added, rather wittily, I thought. I laughed again, but he looked hurt and I felt ashamed.

That was it. How are you taking it? Two in a day. Disgraceful, isn't it? But you know, Ruth, this morning I woke up thinking of Harry and the so many times he'd come back reeking of other women. And all those other tell-tale signs I'd learnt to recognise: the tie knotted differently from when he left, hair still damp from the shower, breath which told of a toothbrush kept somewhere else. It was strange thinking about it, and all the anger I had stored up inside me. I found myself wondering if Harry had sometimes felt just as I had with Kevin – moments of tenderness and love – golden things I hadn't been able to give him. Why was it I couldn't, do you think? And then I thought, if I'd been the woman I am now, would I have done the same as Harry did? Could I have loved him – and I *did* love him – and still done this?

There'll never be an answer, of course. The last chance has gone.

And now? Well, change of tempo, other things have happened since I wrote last. Would you believe I had a visit from Ah-man-dah, actually begging me to release Harry? I almost laughed. 'I don't have any keys,' I said. 'Harry's free to do as he likes.' She looked uncomfortable. I got the feeling that Harry had been doing precisely that, and that was the trouble. Almost certainly he's got some little Baltic tart by now. But what magic did Amanda imagine I could weave? An estranged wife being pleaded to by the one who took him? Absurd! She must be desperate, the silly bitch. And my, her breasts do droop: the hanging gardens of Boobylon.

Now – much more important – my commissions! More of them. Bill the architect wants another mural. Why? Does he really believe I'm good? Should I start believing I'm good? What's more, he has some stinking rich clients on Chelsea Reach who are extremely interested, he says. He's shown them photos of my 'house-boat'. I know you think my glittering art school career was a time utterly wasted, but it's beginning to look as if genius was merely biding its time. Don't you agree that thirty-five is a perfect, mature age for talent to ripen? Anyway, pots of money are rattling just round the corner all of a sudden, plus heavy hints at expenses available for sketching trips. Well, we all know what that means. I wonder if Nina knows it. I hope so, the baggage. I shall enjoy getting one up on her.

Finally, the blizzard has brought some unbelievably rare sparrow to our reservoir at the end of the street, according to Roger the historian. He's had me scanning the frozen reed-beds for a conspicuous white eye-stripe. Jesus, everything's totally white out there as it is; how am I supposed to find any kind of white stripe on something the size of a mouse? Ridiculous business, though hundreds of people don't appear to think so; the whole place is teeming with Bill Oddies laden with cameras and thermos flasks.

Forgive me, I've gone on far too long, and I've said nothing about you and your turmoils. God, how I feel for you at that dinner party. Everyone's nightmare – like slagging off a friend without realising the phone's still connected. There should be an eject button for moments like that.

Hang on a second, doorbell . . . Oh no! A gigantic bunch of roses, and a note, 'Lay, lady lay . . . not a big brass bed, but you're fantastic. Kevin.' By Interflora from next door! Ruth, this is getting too much for me.

Kevin, you're fantastic too. And I hope you can keep my secret.

With love and bewilderment,

Janice.

February 12th

Dear Headmaster,

I greatly appreciate your decision not to expel my son, and of course I shall put it to him that such incidents absolutely must not occur again.

Naturally you are right to say that a marriage break-up is likely to have a disruptive effect on a child of impressionable age. And since I understand from Clive that all his school friends are in a similar position, it must be hard for you having to consider expelling the entire school.

I am delighted that you consider him to be a bright and imaginative boy. I can only suggest that perhaps it was imagination which led him to possess the photographs you say he has been distributing around the school. Boys do seem to mature early these days, don't they? Indeed, smoking in a chapel may be no more than a bid for manliness harnessed to a healthy spirit of rebellion. I do agree, on the other hand, that such behaviour is unacceptable.

The decision to excuse Clive from boxing is one I can only welcome. It can indeed be a dangerous sport, and I trust that the boy in question will make a speedy recovery.

Yours gratefully,
Janice Blakemore.

Hotel Baltic
Vilnius
Lithuania

February 13th

Dear Piers,

This is a hasty letter. I have less than twenty-four hours to get out of the country, and hope the Soviet authorities aren't putting a clamp on mail as they are on honest reporting. I'll write more fully from my underground shelter in Bolton Grove.

There's a universal feeling of shock here. The troops moved in yesterday – conscripts from some Shangri-La republic for the most part – and there was nothing to be done. You could see the helplessness in people's eyes, just as you could see it on your TV screens, no doubt. It was mindless slaughter. What use is a peaceful demonstration when tank commanders are Pavlov's dogs and can't read the placards anyway? With a bunch of other journalists, I watched with a sense of impotent rage and horror tanks breaking human limbs like matchsticks – hard to take marriage bust-ups and domestic squabbles too seriously after that. You know, in all my years of reporting I'd never actually seen anyone killed before. So I am no longer a tenderfoot. We all came back to the hotel numbed and silent. Then some square-headed apparatchik arrived with the order for us to get out. A *Mirror* man, admittedly pie-eyed on vodka, said, 'What the fucking hell for?', and a couple of thugs roughed him up for his pains. Must have made a good headline this morning.

We can all hear the clock ticking loudly backwards.

I'm left with such admiration for people's courage. Not so much in standing up against the Russian tanks, which is just martyrdom. It's more the binding courage of people who can do nothing but wait for their freedom, as many of the Balts have waited for fifty years, and as their children will go on waiting for another fifty if necessary, and still die waiting. It's hard to imagine: never to have what you need most, never to stop believing it the most valuable of things, even if you never live to see it, even if it may never come at all. It's something we hardly think about, take for granted, sell cheaply. It makes me understand nationalism: a corporate self-love – you see it in the gentle granite of their faces. I admire them and hate to leave – for Bolton Grove in particular, and on St Valentine's Day in *most* particular – though that at least will be taken care of, courtesy of the *Washington Post*, whose corn-fed correspondent will be on her (slow) way homewards. I shall hope and pray the Lady Amanda gets no wind of my return. Collision meetings at Heathrow are not recommended.

How goes *la vita diplomatica*? Your paperwork sounds as relentless as the Soviet tanks. Delighted to hear Ruth's reputation for social finesse remains undiminished.

Yours in exile,

Harry.

My darling Clive,

I dare say the headmaster is a wanker, but none the less he *is* the headmaster. Perhaps he does sometimes draw the wrong conclusions, and you and your friends were only trying to film a starling's nest under the eaves; all the same he did find that video camera set up right outside the assistant matron's bedroom window, and he didn't seem to think the video showed too many starlings.

You may also have decided religion's a lot of old phooey, but please try to appreciate that many people don't share that view, and out of respect for them you should understand that a font is for holy water, not yours, and that cannabis is actually illegal, in chapel or anywhere else. You're fortunate that Mr Arnold is innocent enough not to know the difference between tobacco and pot.

Darling, I know it's not easy having to obey petty regulations, but school is supposed to be a place where you're taught things that will be useful to you when you grow up, and certain rules really are necessary or all of you might as well run wild in the street. The law wouldn't allow that, and neither, frankly, would I. So, do please try to behave a little better.

Spindle has become very sweet, but now has a habit of leaping on the bed and purring in my ear just when

I'm dropping off to sleep, the little beast.

The snow's all melted, and Daddy seems to be back in England.

Lots of love,

Mummy.

March

March 3rd

Dear Janice,

Your long letter eventually reached me, having made
a circuit of unknown addresses between here and Piraeus.
That could be because some pigeon appears to have gone
splat right across the address. It could also be that
the contents fired it like an Exocet from one *macho*
household in Athens to another, leaving each in ruins.
I like to think so.

As for your strike rate, if each mural is to be
accompanied by an extra-mural activity, then just five
more will be enough to earn you a permanent place
on the Centre Court. Let me tell you something. If my
great-grandfather – the one who helped raise funds for
the present All England Club – could have known the
destiny of one of his precious debenture seats, he'd have
laughed his head off, being himself a famous bigamist
as well as the sire (so it's said) of fourteen illegitimate

children. Perhaps, my darling, that will make you feel better about Harry – who seems, by the way, to have narrowly missed being pulped by a Russian tank.

Send Kevin out here immediately; our embassy is woefully weak in his skills.

Not so, I have to say, the French embassy, though the skills have yet to be properly tested. I'd imagined after my *faux-pas* at dinner that the diplomatic life held no future for me, and as far as our own dear ambassador is concerned that is undoubtedly so. What I hadn't reckoned on was *la belle France*. It turns out that my little *tête-à-tête* with the French ambassador on that fateful evening quite transported the man, because out of the blue he rang and invited me to the opera. Crafty bastard, his spies must have told him Piers was away visiting our consulate in Salonika. They're so unscrupulous, these French men. I do admire them.

You may not know, but opera in Greece is *comique* without intending to be. *La Traviata* was *La Travestiata*, and the ambassador gallantly suggested we leave after the first interval. I think my Yves Saint-Laurent dress may have prompted this as much as the singing – you remember the one, 'deceptively simple' as they say, in other words, hugs all the right bits. The ambassador's name, incidentally, is Jean-Claude, followed by something complicated full of *de la's* and *ières*, all suggesting ruthless feudal connections and priceless vineyards. Anyway, Jean-Claude took me to a restaurant not far from the opera house where I suspect he's discreetly well-known, judging by the flowers and the miniature bottle of perfume which rapidly appeared on the table. What

I do so love about French men is how seduction is offered as part of their culture – as high art. You think you're having a discussion about Molière, only to realise you've been told about your skin, your hair, your eyes, your smile; and by the time you do realise it he's on to talking about Le Corbusier, and did I know that 'the Corb' actually designed a country retreat for some former French ambassador, and it would give him the deepest pleasure to show it to me one weekend if I chanced to be free? Bravura performance, it was. No touching up. The power of the word – look, no hands!

Well, since I haven't had a whiff of an affair all these months (I don't count Mistra) I can't see myself saying no, can you? Jean-Claude did make a point of mentioning Madame Ambassadeur, and how she frequently felt the need to return to Paris to refresh her spirits, so I don't anticipate any problems there. Now I suppose I simply have to await the call. Piers is so used to me disappearing for the weekend that he won't even notice I've gone.

In fact I was away last weekend – came back only last night. Our own country shack (most definitely *not* by Le Corbusier) which I love. It was earliest spring and the cyclamen were beginning to push up among the rocks. At midday it was warm enough to sit out on the little terrace we've made under a rattan roof. Wobbly wooden chairs from the village – very ethnic, we've become. And – you must believe me – I began to write. No, not letters, not even a diary, but a *book*! Think of that. You with your murals and me with my scribbling; what a pair!

I'd better explain. This new and unexpected turn of

events was another outcome of my dreamy evening with His Excellency Jean-Claude Whatnot-de-la-Something-ière. I made him laugh so much with stories (edited) of my various exploits as a diplomat's wife in different outposts of civilisation, that he suggested I wrote them down. Which is what I started to do last weekend, sitting on my terrace with a bottle of wine in the midday sun, accompanied by a friendly neighbourhood goat who tried to make lunch of my manuscript whenever I went off for a pee. I've called him Nero, not because of his habits but because he's black (you see, I'm managing to learn a little Greek). It's enormous fun recalling all the most awful things that have happened to me since I joined the diplomatic wagon-train, however many years ago it was. I'd almost forgotten some of them – like the time I was bathing naked off a Mexican beach at night, and suddenly the floodlights were turned full on and I found myself in the middle of a BBC wildlife documentary about manatees. It's really a huge tribute to Piers that he's got as far as he has with me around.

Anyway, scribble, scribble. I did two days of it. I've promised Jean-Claude he can read it when it's finished. If I haven't received an invitation for the weekend by then, the book should clinch it, provided of course Madame Ambassadeur doesn't get hold of it first, in which case it could be the end of the Entente Cordiale and early retirement for Piers Conway (which at least would make publication sooner rather than later).

What my scribblings also bring home to me is the sheer absurdity of diplomatic life, as well of course as my own total unsuitability for it. The book has a title, by the way. *Alas in Wonderland*. Will that do? I like it.

You shall see it, naturally, but not before the French ambassador, because in those stakes my need is considerably greater than thine. And anyway, you seem to be doing disgracefully well without any stimulating literature to aid you.

I want to hear more. Your last account was brilliant. Keep it up, as they say.

With love from your kiss-and-tell authoress,

Ruth.

PS You'll be pleased to hear that Piers's piles are better. He insists on referring to them as 'haemorrhoids'. I wish he wouldn't refer to them at all.

Dearest Ruth,

Hey! How about this! I can see it clearly from my window right now. No 3 has a 'For Sale' board outside. And that – in case you haven't done your sums right – is 'Arold and Ivy. I feel like standing in the street shouting, "Roll up, roll up! Bijou residence. Going for a song." Needless to say I shall have my eyes glued. If I see a couple of retired schoolmistresses looking interested I shall tell them it's got dry rot.

How long does it take to sell a house? I must go and enquire at the estate agents. I'm also racking my brains to think of someone I fancy who might be urged to buy it. Don't *you* know anyone? (But why should you cooperate? It's your debenture seat!)

I wonder if Kevin would help; he has my interests at heart. 'No problem, darlin'. Who'd y'like? David Puttnam? Bernardo Bertolucci? John Irvin? Michael Winner?'

Now I'm going to tell you about the party. The one at No 9, Maurice's house: you remember, the invitation which arrived on the morning I invited him to come up to his reputation. 'Maurice and Lottie request . . .', it said, the two names conjoined as I bet they haven't really been for years. God, Harry and I used to send out invitations like that, invariably for a day when we'd just had a mega punch-up, and I'd spend the evening staring glassy-eyed into the claret-cup. Looking back, it's amazing how civilised people can be when they're actually wanting to kill each other.

So I went alone, of course. Dangerous. At least, I hoped so. Actually I was wondering mainly how my *amours* would react. Ignore me? Discuss me among themselves? After all, don't you remember how we always used to talk about how we 'did it', even when we didn't and I never even had, unlike you (Lord, I was envious)? Anyway, there were one or two anxious glances as I entered, mostly from women I didn't know, whose husbands were braying on about gilts or the Glucose account and hadn't even noticed I was there – you knew just looking at them that they could only come thinking about the hundred share index. I felt good. You'd have liked my dress which I bought especially from my 'mural' account. Very simple: white cashmere two-piece, the innocent look but definitely figure-hugging (innocent but not necessarily for long), plus a few Butler and Wilson geegaws – glittery earrings, chunky pearl bracelet. And enough Giorgio to leave a trail of turned heads as I made my way towards Lottie, who was standing next to the buffet smiling painfully. No sign of Maurice; in fact he came nowhere near me all evening.

I'm not actually all that hot at these occasions; I tend to make a splendid entrance and then wonder what I'm supposed to do next. There was also a certain awkwardness in the room because people mostly knew about Harry and thought perhaps they shouldn't, so didn't like to mention it. It was like being at a party with an unwanted ghost.

After I'd run out of silences with Lottie I stood alone for a bit, glass in hand, pretending to gaze hard at a terribly boring painting. And what a lot you pick up: Lottie's look of real fear while Maurice tested the canapés; Kevin's 'researcher for the evening' filching a silver urn from a table of 'artfully arranged knick-knacks'; some redhead trying hard to hide a lovebite on her neck; Nina deliberately dropping her cigarette on the parquet flooring (Maurice swept it up with a look of real loathing – what's up there, I ask?)

The surprise was Ah-man-dah. She seems to have decided to go for the 'sisters under the skin' bit – you know, both of us done wrong by the same bastard, so we have a lot in common. 'I know how hurt you must be, but we ought to talk about it.' She looked a fright for once, in a sort of goose-turd green job that went down at the front and up at the back. 'Nothing to talk about,' I said airily. 'If you're what Harry wants I really do think he'd better have you.' Just then Kevin came up crooning, 'You made me love you; you woke me up to do it.' She didn't know quite how to take that, particularly when he gave me a huge wink. God, I was pleased he was there. He seemed perfectly happy to leave his bimbo going around nicking things. The only trouble was he insisted on putting his arm round me. Fortunately he put his other arm round Ah-man-dah, which took a longer reach, and then pinched her bum which distracted attention from the fingering that was going on on my side. Then I noticed Robert, whom I hadn't set eyes on since our romp on the floor. He gave me a lingering spaniel look and went back to talking to

Nina, who was dressed like a pantomime dame waiting to have her balloons popped. Angus came over gravely and enquired after my lump, then began to stuff his face with quiche to avoid further conversation. His wife ignored me stoically: I wondered if she knew. With an expression like hers you can never tell: permanent disapproval of anyone prettier, which doesn't leave out too many. Then the sweet portrait painter, Ambrose, trapped me in a corner and wittered on about the picture he was going to do of me when the spring flowers were out, and had I thought about what I'd like to wear yet? Little does he know how little. He has a rather beautiful face, in fact, like a Pre-Raphaelite lover gone to seed. His wife, he said, was at a prayer meeting. He looked rescued.

All the others from the street were there too, of course, plus a lot more I didn't know. As the decibel level rose, I wandered off into the kitchen where I met a tubby little man who turned out to be the chairman of the Lambeth Labour Party. I tried not to express surprise at his being there, and fished around for something to say that wouldn't make him think I was one of those Tory ladies who call themselves a Liberal Democrat. Then Courtenay appeared – the would-be Labour MP – and I realised the connection. I hardly knew Courtenay, but he seemed in an effusive mood and a bit pissed. He'd just got adopted as parliamentary candidate for Lambeth, he announced. When the party chairman had gone off to find a drink, he explained with discreet glee that apparently the present Lambeth MP has been caught committing buggery; all hushed up for the moment, but there's no question of his being readopted. So Courtenay at last has a safe seat waiting for him. 'I hope it's safer than your predecessor's,' I said. He looked at me and blinked, then he roared with laughter. I got the feeling that it was the first time a woman had ever cracked a smutty joke at him.

We talked a lot after that. He's one of those suffocatingly good, old-fashioned socialists I thought had died out. You know the type – burning with a kind of innocent fire and a Messianic faith in social equality for all his Oxbridge background, family money, a name like Courtenay Gascoigne and a wife who writes literary novels which heave themselves on to the Booker shortlist before dying a death. We talked about marriage – his and mine. His wife liked to dominate, he explained with a resigned air. She was energetic; she liked to do everything bigger and more often than other people – books, children, 'Food, I'm afraid, too,' he added with a forgiving laugh. 'She has a weight problem.' 'You mean she's greedy,' I said, somewhat rudely. 'Well, perhaps not exactly that, but . . .', and he trailed away into silent agreement. I got the impression socialism was a monastic retreat for him, something she couldn't touch or swallow up.

He rather took to me. My God, the man's lonely. He's roping me in to fund-raising for Romanian children, which gives me an entrée, I suppose, as well as something worthwhile and not entirely self-indulgent to do. All the same, I think I'll make a pitch for him next: a private, fund-raising celebration while Mrs G is hitting page six hundred on the word processor. His eyes, I noticed, were not always on philanthropic horizons. He liked my outfit, he said. He meant he liked my legs.

We were drawn back upstairs by the sound of something exploding. I suggested to Courtenay it was probably one of Nina's breasts bursting, and he gave me a squeeze of pleasure. I wasn't actually so far out: got the anatomy right at least. Ah-man-dah had dropped a jug of hot punch, and as she reached down – totally pissed – one of her boobs fell out, like one of those Italian cheeses. Kevin with great aplomb yelled out, 'Overboard!' and reached down and scooped it back in again. Ah-man-dah seemed beyond noticing, and Robert was trying to steer her towards the door. Then I saw that she was crying. For Harry, I wondered?

I felt strange. Harry used to love parties like that. He liked things to happen, and he'd re-run it afterwards when we got home as though he was reporting for ITN. I often wondered if he was a bit of a sadist, and whether he liked chatting up other women in front of me for the same reason. He'd always insist I look 'elegant'; then he'd spend the entire evening with his hand up a mini-skirt or down a maxi-*décolletage* while I was safely parked with the other 'elegant' wives talking about schools. Do you remember that time you decided to tart me up, and all those roving reporters roved over me while Harry smouldered in a corner? Wow, he looked handsome – and absolutely furious. We fought all the way home, and he accused me – ME! – of wanting an affair. Then he leapt on to me the minute we got into the bedroom. We made so much noise that Clive woke up and wandered into the room. 'What are you doing on

147

top of Mummy?' Poor Harry, all red and bursting. 'Just keeping her warm. GO BACK TO BED.' I did a sketch for him the next day, of a whole lot of sleek men with dogs' heads, all panting for it. 'Newshounds', I called it. Harry used it as a dartboard for ages. The bull's-eye was Our Man at the Kremlin, whom he couldn't stand. Never liked competition, our Harry. Eamonn something, the man was called. He chased me for a while – did I ever tell you? A pretty mild pursuit, 'Here if you ever want it,' sort of thing.

And why didn't I? All those years. Do you think that's why I'm behaving the way I am now? Fury at all those years of self-deception, believing wives should be tolerant and good, and men should be free to haul their ashes. Perhaps I really hate men for putting that one over on me, and I can't rest till I've paid them back.

But I don't hate men, Ruth. I love them, and perhaps I'm only just beginning to understand what they are and how vulnerable they are. I think I've come to regard my debenture seat as a kind of diploma in male studies.

And I have to admit, I'm enormously enjoying studying for it. A crash course in being utterly wicked after so many years of trying to be virtuous. I feel I'm waking up at last, like all the spring flowers in my garden. I love that garden. Every day there are surprises. A splash of purple crocuses opened this morning in the sun, and I stood there smiling at them. There were bees out, too. I'd like to keep bees.

Oh, I must tell you. Len, our postman, told me of a lovely old lady round the corner who takes up dresses. So I went to see her. Lil, she's called. Eighty-six. A real Mrs Tiggy-Winkle. Well, I collected a couple of things from her this morning, and we got talking. Suddenly she asked, 'D'yer read the *Sun*?' And I said, 'No.' 'Well, you ought,' she went on. 'There was this piece on Valentine's Day about what to give yer man, see, and they gave a knitting pattern. For willy-warmers, it was.' 'Oh really,' I said. 'Yeah. So, yer see, I made some. Want to 'ave a look? 'Ere. But they got it wrong, didn't they? No 'ole at the end, and nuffin to tie it round the bag. They're good, aren't they, mine? I oughta know, mind you. I've 'ad three 'usbands, and they're all much the same down there, aren't they? Want one for yer old man? I'll knit yer one.' I didn't like to say I'd kicked my old man out, so I said yes. I think I'll give it to Kevin, so he won't be cold for his bimbos.

Chelsea Reach comes on apace, you'll be happy to hear. Two commissions. Two tycoons with a penthouse each. Bill's right – Shakespeare country is what they want. I wonder if they'd like Lil's willy-warmers, too.

Saw Harry on the box a little while ago, sidestepping the tanks in Lithuania. I felt quite shocked and frightened for him. This worried me a bit. But then I thought, 'Christ, I'm human, aren't I? And I *was* married to the man for twelve years.'

I suppose he must be back in London. I bet he doesn't need a willy-warmer.

I love *Alas in Wonderland*. But will you dare show it to Piers? Yes, knowing you, you probably will. And knowing Piers, he'll probably enjoy it.

More soon.

Lots of love,

Janice.

1 River Mews
London W4

March 10th

Dear Headmaster,

I acknowledge the refund cheque for £3.85, but it must surely be possible to find a different insurance company willing to cover Clive on the school skiing trip. Personally, I cannot see the connection between petty vandalism to church property and possible mishaps on the nursery slopes, and I am glad to hear from you that my husband is insistent on this matter. Without insurance, of course, there can be no question of our son joining the party, and I shall look forward to receiving full reimbursement from the school, including the 'liability loading' surcharge you decided to impose as a condition of taking Clive at all.

On the further matter of discipline which you raise, I appreciate that the school motto underlines the value placed upon alertness at all times; but would you not agree that to be able to compose a pun in Latin, somewhat changing its meaning, is quite an achievement for an eleven-year-old, as well as a healthy tribute to your teaching of the classics? I do agree of course that the school's founder probably did not intend 'alertness' to mean spying on female staff in the privacy of their bedrooms. But could the school not provide curtains, as well as see to it that builders' ladders are not left in place at night to tempt enterprising children to make use of them?

I should also like to point out that the camera in question was not Clive's – he does not possess such a thing. Nor, as far as I am aware, does he have access to any marketing company which may have expressed interest in purchasing the offending videotape.

I am delighted to hear that Clive's end-of-term examinations have proved more than satisfactory. I am proud of him.

Yours very sincerely,

Janice Blakemore.

March 14th

Dear Piers,

A muffled voice from the *reichsbunker*. Why does one invariably come back to a sea of troubles? I'm threatened with East Germany very soon. Hasten the day.

First, I find myself plunged into turmoils with Clive's wretched school. Why on earth did we send him there? They behave as though *Tom Brown's Schooldays* had never been written. Mind you, I get the impression Devil's Island might find it hard to deal with Clive. The trouble is, the kid's bright, and in ten years' time I can see him following in your august footsteps in a blaze of academic honours and an Armani suit. In the meantime, what's to be done? Maybe puberty will slow him up a bit.

Because of all this I felt I had to ring Janice. She agreed to meet, and we had a pub lunch at The Dove on the river at Hammersmith. Her choice; it made me feel distinctly uncomfortable considering the number of liaisons I've begun there. I had a vision of them all turning up at the same time.

It was strange seeing her. To my surprise she looked younger – serene, very pretty. I didn't know whether to be pleased or disappointed. Her perfume reminded me of so many times I'd fancied her, and it was disturbing to realise I was hoping she'd say, 'You know, we could talk more privately at home', and we could have ended up in bed. I even tried the charm bit. It always used to work, even when I didn't mean it and was in the middle of a hot-and-heavy with someone else. This time I did mean it, and all she said was, 'Do you think we could settle it then? Does he stay at this school or not? I'd rather like to get back to my painting.'

Christ, she's working, Piers. Janice *working*. Earning money, too. It's an uncomfortable feeling when you think someone ought to be miserable because of you, and they're not. I suddenly felt at an acute disadvantage. And you know how it is, when you feel you're losing something you have an irresistible urge to play all the cards in your hand, even though you know there's absolutely no point. I did just that. We were walking back through the public gardens by the river, and I asked her whether she'd thought about all the things I'd said in my letter – about loving her and missing our life together and trying to put it right. And she said, yes, she had thought about it a lot, and she was inclined to think I'd always been right; that I was the sort of person who needed affairs, and why not? So it was all for the best now, wasn't it, she suggested. There was no longer a problem.

Which wasn't what I'd meant at all.

Then she said, 'I think we'd better stop here. I don't want people to think you've come back.' She didn't say it unkindly. 'It'll be easier when we sell the house,' she added, 'but if you don't mind I'd rather not have another upheaval right now. I'm just finding my feet. How about you – are *you* all right?' I said yes, I was fine, which wasn't strictly true. 'I'm glad,' she went on and she touched my arm and gave me a warm smile, 'because I'm really not angry with you any more. And now I must go.'

So there we are. I've made such a balls-up of things, Piers. After I left Janice that afternoon I came back to my rabbit-hole and had a red-hot screw with our correspondent for the *Washington Post* – who left this morning for the States – and all I could think about as we lay there afterwards was whether Liverpool was going to win the FA Cup and whether John Barnes was likely to be fit to play on the wing.

Oh well, Dresden here I come. Plunge back into work. And maybe – who knows? – one of these fine days I may find someone I can screw and live with at the same time. Or someone who can put up with me as I am.

Salonika sounded extremely dreary. Not as dreary, I assure you, as No 3a Bolton Grove.

All the best,

Yours,

Harry.

ATHENS 1600 HRS MARCH 16
CABLE DESPATCH TO: BLAKEMORE
1 RIVER MEWS LONDON W4 UK
BASTILLE FALLEN STOP RUTH

Dearest Ruth,

I need to tell you a story. Are you ready?

Right! Yesterday morning. Breakfast as usual, reading the paper, French windows open – a spring morning that was like summer. I was happy. I had work to do. I'd coped with Harry better than I could ever have believed – we'd met to sort out problems with Clive's school. And then the phone went. It was Roger – you know, No 5, the historian bird freak. Would I please come bird-watching with him? This evening, perhaps? The light would be perfect then, and the early spring migrants might have arrived in this warm weather. (What the hell was a 'spring migrant'? I had visions of a Breton onion-seller with wings.)

Now, there have already been quite a number of perishing hours with Roger by the old reservoir, in the company of the woolly-hat-and-binocs brigade. What's more, I'd been hoping to get on with Kevin's 'Van Eyck' before Clive turned up on his way skiing. But there was something so eager about Roger's voice, and I didn't feel like disappointing him. He's very sweet – awkward and shy, terribly earnest; he must bruise easily. And that dipso wife can't help. So I said, 'All right,' and I looked out Harry's binoculars as a reminder.

When I turned up it was obvious he'd been waiting for this moment all day. He was so nervous he could barely look at me. He was anxious to show me a discovery he'd made, he said; that the reservoir was once a trout pond in Elizabethan times, even earlier. He'd found documents, he said. There used to be a Tudor manor house here – and he showed me where he believed the walls would have been, a low ridge – and over there was the smokery, he was quite sure. He was trying to get London University to organise a dig. 'Not in the migration season, of course; mustn't disturb the birds.' And he laughed.

His little joke seemed to give him courage, and he actually looked at me. 'May I just say, you're looking very lovely?' I murmured a surprised thank you. 'Oh no,' he said hastily, 'I should be the one to thank *you*.'

He had the expression of a little boy with a new train set, and I wondered what was coming next. Then suddenly it was, 'Look! I told you. Keep still.' And the binoculars were up. 'They *are* here. Reed warblers, in mid-March; so early. All the way from Africa, the little darlings – think of that. Take a look. There!' I did as I was told and peered through my binoculars at the reeds. But I kept turning the focussing thing the wrong way, and when I eventually got it right the lenses steamed up. 'See them? Look, there they are again.' The binoculars kept wobbling about and my arms were aching. I couldn't even see the reeds, let alone a bird. 'What's a reed whatnot look like?', I whispered. 'There it is. Look. Flying. *On* the reeds. See it? Oh, it's gone. No, there it is again. Let me try and show you.' And he came round behind me and tried to guide my binoculars with his arms round my shoulders. I noticed his hands, smooth from handling ancient manuscripts, and with beautifully manicured nails. He smelled warm like toast. Then I got hiccups.

I thought he might be angry. There was a swan floating close by, and I said hopefully, 'Look, there's a swan.' But he didn't seem to notice either the swan or the hiccups. It was beginning to grow dusk, and the light on the water was soft and gentle. By now Roger was bubbling with enthusiasm. 'They're probably nesting just here. They bind their nests right into the reeds, you know. Perhaps we can find it. It means waiting a bit to see where they fly to. Let's keep watch from the hide along there.' I had often noticed this shed-like thing with flaps at the front and wondered what it might be. Roger led the way, me slithering and trying to stifle the hiccups. It was dark inside the hide, and I could hear him muttering to himself about needing to open the flaps just a little so as not to disturb anything. I took a step forwards and tripped over a wooden bench with a crash. I imagined the birds would have been scared all the way back to Africa. But again Roger didn't appear to notice, and at least it stopped the hiccups.

There were two flaps which he opened about a foot, and we sat one by each, side by side on the wooden bench, elbows planted on the ledge with our binoculars raised and gazing out into the dusk. I felt like someone out of an old spy film. There wasn't a soul to be seen – and not a bird either, for that matter. The bench was cold to the bum. I didn't think Roger was having much luck with his warbler's nest either, because every now and then he gave out a despondent grunt. It wasn't just the tedium. I gradually got the feeling he was staring through his binoculars searching for something he was bursting to tell me. It was like those silences at one's first dance. How could I break it?

'Does your wife watch birds?', I asked eventually, realising it was a ridiculous question the moment I asked it. Roger lowered his binoculars and gazed at me. He had such an appealing, sad face; bird-watching even made him *look* like a small boy. 'Goodness, no!', he said. 'She doesn't do anything I like – ever. That's why it's good to have you here. So very good.' Suddenly he placed his hand on mine: oh, the effort it must have cost him. 'You're such a beautiful creature.' He sort of gulped as he said it.

Then he poured it out. He loved me. I was a goddess. Ever since he'd first set eyes on me . . . he hoped I didn't mind. He expected nothing, of course; just the occasional expedition like this. 'A bird in the hide?', I asked. He gulped again and smiled nervously. 'No, a bird of paradise,' he said, and I laughed. 'In that case I should be a dowdy little creature, shouldn't I? The male bird's got the gorgeous feathers. I'm the one who waits for the handsome prince's favours.' He looked all wondrous, as if he was trying hard to believe it. There was another gulp, then, 'You know, I shouldn't really say this, but I do dream sometimes of being able to do you favours. Of loving you – totally.' His face seemed frightened suddenly, in case I laughed at him. 'You mean, make love to me? Would you like to?' He just hung his head. 'Oh, my lovely girl, oh . . . oh my goodness. I'd, I'd be too overwhelmed. I . . . couldn't.' 'Are you sure?', I persisted brazenly. 'You could always try.' 'Oh no, no. Nothing like that has happened for many years, I assure you. But thank you, thank you. Such kindness. And such beauty.'

I was just thinking, 'Christ, the man can't be much more than fifty,' when I heard a loud squawk from somewhere down in the reedbed outside. It was as if Roger had touched an electric wire. His body gave a terrific jolt. 'What on earth is it? Sounds like something being sick,' I said.

Roger was by now feverishly scanning the reedbed in the darkness with his binoculars. 'It can't be!', he kept exclaiming. 'It's not possible, you never find them here.' The sound went on – a raucous chuck-chuck-chuck. Utterly undistinguished, you'd have thought. Not to Roger, it wasn't. 'It has to be,'he said in a tone of amazement, 'Cetti's Warbler! Wait till the Royal Society hear about this. Quite impossible to mistake that call.'

What was also impossible to mistake was its effect on Roger. His face was radiant, even in the dark. He seemed twenty years younger – a man transformed, every part of him – rampant. He must have been saving it up all those years. My dear Ruth, I'll leave the rest to your imagination. But I shall never again judge a bird by his feathers. I swear to you, my gentle historian came to the mating call of Cetti's Warbler.

And that was how the twitcher twitched.

Oh, your cable has just arrived. *Vive la France*! I bet he wasn't half as loud as Cetti's Warbler.

Love in hiding. And five down!

Janice.

69 Damaskinou
Neapolis
(Athens)

March 24th

Dear Janice,

Two letters from you were waiting when I got back on Sunday. Piers had opened the first by mistake and then read it on purpose, the bastard. He revelled in your account of the party, and went on about your figure-hugging cashmere two-piece to such an extent that I denied him marital rights – a poor excuse, but I had just spent a week with Jean-Claude and was in no mood for further engagements. Oh by the way, he wants a willy-warmer (Piers, that is); the trouble is, knowing him he'll forget to take it off, which could make marital rights even less likely.

Now, I suppose you want to know about the French ambassador (thank God you didn't mention him in your letter; that's definitely *not* one for a husband's ears, at least not until it's over, which I hope won't be yet).

Well, Monsieur didn't waste time. Madame flew off to Paris to nurse ailing relatives (long may they ail) and Jean-Claude decided he 'needed' a spring holiday. By coincidence I needed to get away too ('What, again?', said Piers). So I found myself installed in the famous Le Corbusier country retreat I told you about – not far from Mycenae as it turned out (which we visited, of course). It wasn't quite the consummation devoutly to be wished since we'd already had that the week before (hence my cable) – in the French embassy, to be exact. I call the country retreat 'famous', which I shouldn't because it isn't. What I'm trying to say is that Le Corbusier was famous enough, but this particular child of his genius doesn't appear in any of the official tomes for the simple reason that he disowned it. Evidently the ambassador for whom he built it in the 1950s led a private life which would make Jean-Claude's seem celibate. His Excellency was determined to secure the most celebrated architect of the day, but didn't see eye to eye with the Corb when it came to such details as interior swimming-pools, fountains, walls angled to receive cunningly-placed mirrors, sunken marble baths and the like. Purity of line had one meaning for the architect and quite another for the ambassador. So in mid-construction the two parted company with some acrimony – Jean-Claude showed me the correspondence which he's inherited. The result is a bizarre mixture of the Ronchamp chapel and a Moroccan harem. I loved it. No rubies in the navel, but luxurious comfort of a raffish kind. Spectacular views over the Bay of Argos, and not another house in sight.

Jean-Claude is a delight, and if I weren't so wise I'd fall in love with him. Most women do, it seems. He's a man to relish and forget. I may find it harder than I'd like to do the latter; the world feels greyer now that I'm not with him.

How can a lover be quite so civilised, I ask myself? As you know, I don't think of myself as civilised at all, certainly not in these matters. I'm a slut when it comes to passions, and a barbarian in most other respects. My only redeeming features are that I say what I think and ask for what I want, both of which land me in a heap of trouble. Perhaps I have a few other virtues, come to think of it: I value friendships (yours of course), I weep easily, I have a thousand appetites, and I love tennis. But civilised I am not. Jean-Claude's centuries-deep polish leaves me feeling like a clod of earth which the servants forgot to remove from the carpet. Yet when he brought me a cognac on the terrace and stroked my shoulders I felt like the Queen of Sheba.

Heigh-ho! *Alas in Wonderland* indeed. This episode will make a sweeter chapter than most. By the way, your delicious tale of the twitching historian brought back to me a night I once spent in Chartres with a medieval historian (couldn't be the same one, surely) who could only come to the striking of the cathedral bell – on the hour, all night (well, nearly). Piers capped that by telling me of a girl he once knew who could only be roused by a particular aria in *Tosca*. It never failed, he said, except that she would insist on hearing the whole thing through, and since the aria was late in the opera this meant hours and hours of foreplay until he discovered how to make the LP leap vast passages and then stick at just the right moment. This was before he met me, he swears, to which my spirited response was that my night of campanology in Chartres might have been 'pre-Piers' too, had he not cradle-snatched me before I'd had a chance to learn about life. He looked doubtful, then confessed he'd made the whole story up, which made me feel even worse, the louse.

I had to tell him about our 'bet', I'm afraid, since he'd been such a shit as to read your letter. But I've sworn him to secrecy; I know he writes to Harry, and a leak in that direction is the last thing you need. I gather your Don Juan is now in Dresden, still I hope nursing the bruises you inflicted at your meeting. Well done! I also gather that the florid Amanda is out of favour, and that at least one tart has come and gone the way of all flesh since her brief reign.

Janice, you are so well out of it. I'm sure it's not always easy: twelve years is a deep well of memories, and there must be many moments of thirst. But things *will* work out for you. Your 'Diploma in Male Studies', as you put it, is also a kind of exorcism, isn't it? An undoing. By the time we meet on the Centre Court the sun will be out and you'll be ready to blossom again.

Talking of which, the hillsides here are bright with spring flowers. Jean-Claude and I walked for hours in the hills among carpets of them. Greece can be beautiful; but perhaps I was seeing it through the eyes of the man who was holding my hand. (God, how sentimental I'm becoming.)

And Kythira? Any chance? Your 'mural account' can't all be going on Clive's skiing trip and alluring outfits to disturb the neighbours' wives. Do try. I miss our company. Letters are fine for confessions and gossip but I should love to sit and talk about all the other things that matter. And don't forget we have a house by the sea – courtesy of the Cretan Bank – for whenever you want, if Cetti's Warbler can spare you.

Fifty pages of *Alas* done. Oh, it's fun. I tell Piers he may read it on the condition he promises not to sue. He says if he was that kind of person he'd have sued me years ago – which I think is probably true.

Now I have to change for some ghastly event celebrating Anglo-Hellenic cultural exchanges – which probably means the British Council is planning to dump yet another Henry Moore exhibition on the Greeks as a sop for not returning the Elgin Marbles. Piers has to give a speech. I am ordered to keep my mouth securely shut.

Oh, how I enjoy the diplomatic way of death.

(I bet you've never made love in a fountain.)

With *my* love to you,

Ruth.

April

                              1 River Mews
                              London W4

                              April 1st

Dear Headmaster,

You asked me to speak to my son before the
beginning of term concerning the incident during the
school skiing trip, and indeed I had a serious talk with
him yesterday.

He feels – and I have to say I'm inclined to agree
with him – that overmuch has been made of a lively
schoolboy prank. Obviously I can't speak for myself
in this matter, but I do remember as a child that one
of the ways my brother and his schoolmates used to
celebrate winter was to hold competitions to see who
could make the most impressive mark in the snow, using
the equipment God gave them. It was not unusual for
them to inscribe their names in this fashion.

It does seem from what Clive has told me that
nothing more grave than this was taking place on the
final evening of the trip, when they were no doubt in
high spirits. It was perhaps unfortunate and tactless of

the boys to inscribe the names of school staff rather than their own, though I'm sure any linkage between those names by means of graphic designs must have been the result of poor draughtsmanship rather than malicious intent. Clive has never excelled at drawing, and the male organ, particularly before puberty, cannot be said to be an efficient instrument in this respect. Besides, we are not talking about indelible graffiti; I imagine the next fall of snow will have obliterated all cause for embarrassment to the masters and mistresses concerned.

I trust next term will proceed more smoothly, and I have had stern words with Clive about this.

Thank you for including details of the school Founder's Day in June, and the kind invitation to attend. I hope to be able to.

Yours sincerely,

Janice Blakemore.

Dear Piers,

For the first time – not to have to write *East*
Germany. An extraordinary feeling for a spy who's
been coming into the cold for fifteen years; especially
so since the East-West divide is actually more in evidence
now than it ever was before the wall came down. Your
remarks on the new Euro-Greeks tapping off EC subsidies into Swiss bank accounts would find plenty of
echoes here, I assure you, except that it's not greasy
politicians on the make but Euro-vultures from Frankfurt and Düsseldorf: they descend hourly out of the
sky. 'Investment' is the buzz-word, meaning 'take-over'.
You can see it at a glance from my hotel window. Each
morning there are more sleek black Mercedes edging out
of the battered Trabants along the quayside of the Elbe
('making Elbe room', grins the man from the FT). All the
West Germany fat-cats seem to be staying here, bustling
around the hotel lobby, flashing American Express gold
cards and smoking cigars no one locally can buy or even
afford if they could. Altogether there's an air of George
Grosz about the place, with no lack of pliant fräuleins
happy to unite East and West in the most lucrative way
they know. The Grosser Garten has acquired a new
meaning since the influx of management from Siemens

and VW. Everywhere it's contracts at boardroom and bawdroom level. Resentment smoulders in the faces of the ordinary people in the street, who know they're being plucked like battery hens by big brother from the West, and can do fuck-all about it. 'Join us, join us,' is the message beamed at them – taken pretty badly by the machine-tool operators whose skills have overnight become about as relevant as Welsh coracle making. The most pitiful specimens are the former party officials who have no skills at all except the exercise of power and privileges now removed. They wander around in unpressed suits like the clergy of a disbanded church. They, at least, deserve it, and no one gives a fuck about them.

Well, there's the former East Germany for you in one paragraph: a great deal longer than the reports I'm required to give on this joyfully reunited nation. United it is; joyful it is not.

I've come to realise rather late in life that newsworthy things only happen in parts of the world one would do anything to avoid. This makes a journalist like me fated to tour a grey world looking for colour. Absurd, isn't it? You on the other hand pass your life in the sunniest and most colourful places, making them all grey. Could we not strike a deal, whereby you add colour to your life by finding me succulent stories, in return for which I can then enjoy the self-indulgent places the Foreign Office sends you to?

You gush about the beauties of spring in the mountains as if you were a born-again Vita Sackville-West. Anemones and cyclamen, indeed. Of course I'm bloody envious. I should adore to be walking in the Greek hills among flowers. Christ, in Poland it was raining. In Romania it was industrial smog. In Lithuania it was cold enough to freeze your balls off. Spring here in Dresden is a billowing of uncollected garbage along the historic terraces of the Elbe. And in London I'm underground. What a truly wonderful life, perfect for keeping body and soul apart. And me, of course, apart from my family.

I've never heard you speak of Ruth as a 'dilettante' before. I wish I could be one: where the bee sucks. At least my life is on the wing. Jutta, who was with me last night (a beautiful panther of a woman), had a husband who was a party boss. He shot himself a month ago. She didn't love him, she said. What a thing to be told over breakfast.

Yours in a time-warp,

Harry.

Dearest Ruth,

If I send Piers a willy-warmer, will you kindly ask your French ambassador if he has a colleague – a *chargé d'affaires*, perhaps – who badly needs a holiday in London (or, even better, would like to buy 'Arold's 'ouse in River Mews)? Tell him, please, that I can't offer Le Corbusier, nor fountains or sunken baths, but the view of the graveyard is a bit special, and he might like the cat. He might also like my seventh veil. I do cook rather well, too, and would be happy to provide *tarte maison* as often as he wishes.

As for you, walking among fields of spring flowers hand in hand, really Ruth, I would never have believed it. You must be smitten. Clearly it has to be you, not me, who rises naked from the foam in Kythira. All right, I know you're not petite and blonde, and that Aphrodite probably wasn't Jewish, but why give in to cultural prejudice? As a matter of fact, since Aphrodite was only a couple of generations away from the very first humans on earth, she was probably a hairy ape-woman; she certainly had a lot to do with *homo erectus*, if my reading of Robert Graves is correct.

As you can see, I'm in a thoroughly silly mood and you don't have to read the rest of this letter if you don't want to. But I feel bubbly because work is going so incredibly well. While you scribble away at

Alas in Wonderland, I'm making great progress with Kevin's 'Van Eyck'. The landscape is actually a copy – well, an adaptation – of the original in the Louvre (I've got a full-size reproduction of the original pinned up in my studio – yes, *studio*, of which more in a minute). Kevin's gone away on a film recce for a week, so he simply left me his house keys, which was trusting of him considering how valuable his kinky collection of paintings is supposed to be. Stupidly I told him my vulgar idea of putting a topless Virgin Mary in the foreground, and of course he leapt at the suggestion, insisting it be a self-portrait. I refused. Can't have his bimbos commenting on what small tits I've got. He looked peeved and said I ought to move in with him and then there wouldn't be any bimbos. 'Rubbish,' I said, and reminded him that he was married already and so was I. He just grinned and said, 'Easy to forget, isn't it?'

Now, the studio. I decided I needed one since I'm seriously in business these days. I tell myself with amazement, 'I'm a professional.' Bill's got me five grand each for the two Chelsea Wharf murals. 'Got yer dirt cheap, darlin'', was Kevin's reaction. 'Tell 'em to fuckin' well double it. Occidental Oil? A hundred grand's just pissin' in a bucket for them. Where's yer self-respect, girl?' But Bill advises moderation: there'll be plenty more commissions if these go down well, he says. And Jesus Christ, ten thousand pounds! I've never dreamt of earning that much. I don't think the Acton Leisure Centre will see my junk stall for a while.

Anyway, so I commandeered Harry's old study. No north light and stuff, only the graveyard view from the basement. But never mind; for the first time in my life I have a real work place of my own. A place that's entirely mine, where I can be and dream, play music, doodle and draw, get drunk if I want, mess up if I want, work all night if I want. And nobody can interrupt, complain, or criticise what I do. It's my palace, my little kingdom, and what's so marvellous is that ideas emerge there as if they've been waiting all these years to be born.

I made an expedition to Rowneys and bought a whole lot of new paint, new brushes, sketchbooks, canvas and lovely gadgets I'll probably never use. I felt so proud. 'May we carry them to your car for you, madam?' 'Yes, if you would be so kind, young man,' I didn't quite say, but looked it, I hope. A bit of a let-down, coming home to do a pastiche of a Van Eyck and then phoning Bill to arrange when I might go and draw the Forest of Arden and Ann Hathaway's cottage, but never mind. I'm a 'real artist', Kevin insists. 'Michael fuckin' Angelo, darlin'. Great legs, too.' Well, I have got good legs, haven't I?

Now to the major event of the year in River Mews. The vicar – who no one's ever met – has made a planning application to build desirable residences on the tennis courts next to the old graveyard. Apparently it's church land. Well, you can imagine the uproar. Nina's in her element both as a tennis player and as the white knight of noble causes. Hell knows no fury, etc. (The vicar's called the Rev Hope, by the way, and is being abandoned by all.) So, Nina called a meeting at No 7 a few days ago. All five of my 'exs' were there, which shows solidarity. Courtenay was elected chairperson and I was co-opted as secretary – proposed by one of my lovers and seconded by another. The outcome was that we formed a residents' association, which Courtenay as a politico knows all about. He also knows our local Labour MP and is going to get to work on him, with me as pretty little assistant there to bat my eyelids and take notes.

But let me tell you more about the meeting. Nina launched it with a passionate tirade against church greed: 'Is this in the spirit of the gospels?' – which I'm sure she's never read. She waved her hands about so much all the diamonds on her fingers flashed in the light. Dr Angus left the meeting in a huff, followed by Ivy (Mrs 'Arold) in her dark glasses and turd-coloured dungarees unzipped to the waist to reveal – I have to say – nothing at all. The poached egg syndrome. She was also wearing two gigantic silver hooped earrings which on her little pin-head made her look exactly like a game of hoop-la on legs, where the two hoops had missed. After that other voices were raised. Ambrose's wife (the walking prayer-mat) thought the issue was spiritual versus material values (Tennis! Spiritual values?) Lottie, Maurice's wife, started to say something in reply which nobody could understand, then stopped in mid-muddle and sat down as if she'd been punctured. Maurice put on his, 'Oh God,' expression. Roger the twitcher made a timid plea for the privacy of his migrant birds on the reservoir, which no one listened to. And at that juncture Ah-man-dah swept in behind a spinnaker of taffeta and a skirt that would have qualified her for the unFastnet race. Kevin, who was sitting next to me and was by now rather pissed on Nina's wine, announced in a stage-whisper, ''Ere come two of Roger's migratin' tits', which everyone pretended not to hear. I said something so ineffectual I can't even remember it, except that everyone seemed to agree with me; finally various motions were carried empowering Courtenay and I to do what we could to pull strings and influence people, and Kevin broke the meeting up sharply with, 'Let's get the fuck out of 'ere.' 'Such an uncouth man,' was Courtenay's wife's sole contribution to the evening. Perhaps the event will be given some significant meaning in her latest novel, page 674.

Courtenay now has an excuse to ring me up and call round for coffee without asking permission of Mrs Lady-Novelist, and we have a jolly time discussing everything but the endangered tennis courts. He treats me like a luxury item, to which I'm not averse. My bet will suffer no setback there, for sure. Whenever he looks at me his face is a battleground for two warring factions, the do-gooder and the lecher.

It all makes me feel a dangerous subversive. There's no doubt about it, to be passively available offers a threat few men seem equipped to deal with, unlike women who find it no problem at all, since men make themselves available all the time. But what am I doing telling you this when you've known it most of your life, haven't you? Do you remember when we did Latin together and had to learn Caesar's little self-congratulatory, 'Veni, Vidi, Vici', and we'd turn it round to make, 'I saw, I conquered, I came'? The trouble is, it now seems to me, where there's no conquering to be done there's a serious problem about coming. Ah well, I'm learning.

You'll have noticed that since I got embroiled in *The Church* v. *River Mews*, my mind has taken a more epistolary turn. And so I have to tell you about the Rev Hope's latest bid to win over the local football crowd. A notice on the church board reads, 'You always score with Jesus'. Pity He doesn't live in River Mews.

To my relief Clive is being good for once. At least I think so: he's been back at school nearly a week without a single phonecall or letter of complaint. I fended off the last broadside from the headmaster (pompous ass) with a tongue-in-cheek reply dated April 1st. I doubt he'll have seen the joke. At least it's the cricket season now – something he takes desperately seriously on account of Harry, who used to play for some team called the Minor Counties which never sounded exactly olympian to me although Harry used to speak of it with awe and even get me to go and watch him. God, the mystique, the tedium and the rain. Will I ever forget those afternoons?

Ah, more visitors to 'Arold's 'ouse, I see. Oh Lord, very seedy-looking. Retired bank manager who plays bowls, certainly. If they come back again I'll treat them to my doomwatch report: death-watch beetle, dry rot, aircraft noise, demolition threat.

Now to my studio. I so love it. I've promised Kevin that I'll finish his mural (*sans* madonna) by his return next week.

Yes, Harry seems to be in Dresden, and looking disgustingly glamorous on the box. You know, in spite of everything it still sickens me to know that every bloody time he appears on the box a hundred thousand little hearts go flutter. They even write to him enclosing their photos, the brazen hussies. And all I've got is Nos 1 to 10, River Mews.

Lots of love,

Janice (Hon Sec, River Mews Residents' Association).

PS I've tracked down the Rev Hope. His front garden is festooned with washing-lines like a cat's-cradle. Kevin calls it the Knickerage.

1 River Mews

April 16th

Clive darling,

Wonderful news that you're in the school cricket team and that you beat Frampton Manor by such a huge score, with you getting all those wickets. I'm so proud. You must be a hero.

This makes me a bit puzzled why Mr Lindwall (is he the sports master?) should have felt the need to telephone me over the weekend. I don't pretend to know a thing about cricket (I leave that to Daddy), but tell me, is there anything actually wrong in getting batsmen out in the way he described? He used the word 'bodyline', which you must explain to me. It did sound rather dangerous, I admit, but I assume it's a batsman's job to get his head out of the way if he's any good, and if he isn't he shouldn't be playing. I said this to Mr Lindwall but he didn't seem to agree.

He also said a couple of other things I didn't understand. Something about, 'roughing up the pitch' and – this really mystified me – 'going to the loo to make the ball square'. I may be a complete idiot, but how can going to the loo make a cricket ball square? I'd have thought it would merely make it wet. And what's the point of having a square ball anyway? Mr Lindwall seemed to think you'd deliberately trodden on it. In the loo? I said this had to be quite absurd, and that it sounded like a pure accident to me. I've often trodden on things in the loo by mistake; it's what comes of having to take your knickers down. We all know how easily things fall out of pockets.

Anyway, I was rather cross with him, especially as I was trying to finish the painting you saw over Easter – for Kevin next door: you know, the one with the winding river and huge landscape. It's been tremendous fun, and soon I've got to start two others for those oil millionaires in Chelsea. Next week in fact I go up to Stratford to do some sketching of Shakespeare places, so wish me luck and fine weather. Bill the architect, who got me the job, is probably going to be there, too; there's some office block he's designed which he needs to visit. So I may have company in the evenings, which will be nice.

You remember they elected me secretary of our new residents' association to stop the Rev Hopeless – as you called him – building houses on the tennis courts. Well, it's proving quite time-consuming, which I don't really like, though I'm enjoying working with Mr Gascoigne, who uses my telephone at all hours trying to persuade MPs, councillors and local bigwigs to oppose the scheme. Apparently Mrs G won't let him use the phone at home because it wakes up the children.

The only other piece of news is that Ambrose – you know, the rather grand Royal Academician – is going to paint my portrait next month. You made caustic remarks about my being the goddess of flowers, I seem to remember. But just you wait! Fame. Fame. All the same, I hope he won't take too long over it because I'm suddenly frantically busy – which is lovely.

Delighted to hear that work's going well. You always did like biology. I trust the frogs were dead.

And don't forget suntan lotion if you're going to play a lot of cricket.

Lots and lots of love,

Mummy.

Dear Piers,

Your letter arrived yesterday, handed to me by the surly hotel receptionist. His grievance is at having to survive now without the perks which the KGB and the CIA have been paying him for years. Jutta tells me he used to run a successful line in pimping for one side and informing for the other – she didn't say which was which – and she should know since her late husband, a senior party official, used to profit from both.

To the main business: I'm totally taken aback. Do British diplomats often send letter bombs? Presumably you have access to secret documents, i.e., letters from J to Ruth? She must tell you something of what's in them, and being a diplomat you're buggered if you're going to disclose what you know. Swine!

But here you are, seriously suggesting I have a good chance of getting back together with Janice. I'm utterly confused by the thought that her coolness when we met in London was just pride and an unwillingness to be hurt again. If she's really been saying that to Ruth then presumably it's true; but has she, or are you inventing it? After reading your letter I spent much of yesterday turning it all over in my mind. I ended up with two issues at least on my side. How much do I really love and want Janice? And how much do I value my freedom? The two are linked crucially. If I value my freedom more, then I don't really want Janice at all. And if I do want her, freedom is of little importance. Freedom to screw around is mostly what it comes down to, and as I blunder into middle age I'm aware that the romance of conquest dies more and more rapidly. I grow bored more easily; and at this rate it'll end with a seedy old Blakemore attempting one-night-stands, scarcely able to raise a stand at all. How lonely and depressing that picture is. I think of Janice, and it hurts.

Then, not content with that bombshell, you drop two more. The offer of your flat off Parliament Hill is unbelievably generous. Yes please, and eternal gratitude. As I told you on the phone last week, I never for one moment expected my lords and masters to give me six months' leave of absence to write a book. OK, it's without pay, but the advance from my publishers will more than make up for that, and it has to be true that if ever there was a moment for a book about Eastern Europe, this is it. I fear it's unlikely to be as entertaining as the undiplomatic memoirs of Ruth Conway, from what you tell me, but at least its publication won't impale you on the Official Secrets Act.

Living in your flat to write it will be a dream. I can't wait to clear out of my underground bunker in Bolton Grove. And Christ, daylight! Civilisation! Warmest thanks, my old friend. And by the way, finding somewhere else for Wimbledon fortnight while Ruth's in London presents no problem at all. I'm not one of her favourite people, and it's the least I can do.

Now, to your third bombshell. Whatever gave you the idea of making it a bet – and a bet, what's more, you know I couldn't refuse? If you'd like a formal and binding acceptance, here it is. 'I, the undersigned Harry S Blakemore, formerly of Dresden and all points east, agree on this day, April 21st, to receive membership of the Marylebone Cricket Club from June of the present year on the condition of an established reunion with my lawful wedded wife Janice, not later than the end of the said month. Signed, HS Blakemore. To be countersigned by P Conway, First Secretary, Her Britannic Majesty's Embassy, Athens.'

Will that do? I can't imagine how I'm going to pull this off. Nor can I imagine how it should be in your power to fix membership of a club other people go blind and ga-ga waiting to get into. Perhaps I'd better not know whose wife you're screwing or whose husband you're blackmailing. In my mind I'm already basking in the pavilion at Lord's in that atrocious tie, surrounded by crimson-faced geriatrics talking of Hobbs and Ranjitsinji. Open beside me is a Fortnum and Mason lunch hamper with smoked salmon, *pâté en croute* and a bottle of chilled Chablis, while below me David Gower is carving the West Indian fast bowlers elegantly to pieces. I am the definition of a happy man.

A bet, then, it is.

On lighter matters, Ruth certainly seems to be living up to her reputation again. But I have to say it's clearly all your fault. If you order your beloved wife to keep her mouth shut at some pompous diplomatic occasion then you shouldn't be surprised if she shuts her eyes too, and people who shut their eyes are liable to snore. Besides, I'm sure it was the most appropriate response to the verbiage no doubt being uttered by the Greek Minister of Culture, even if this wasn't the view of the lady in question. She should have stuck to singing *Never on Sunday*. In any case, the Greek government's got one foot in the grave and the other on a bar of soap, and if it should fall to the sound of Ruth snoring, who's to say this wasn't the most fitting adieu?

I'll be in touch as soon as I get to London. I must say I've enjoyed Dresden in a dark way, and I shall take away with me some bitter-sweet predictions for those I've come to know here. The ex-party boss who haunts the beer halls in a crumpled suit will shortly find that the concession for US porno videos causes him no ideological pain. Our hotel receptionist will discover his contacts to be far more marketable among Japanese trade delegations than they ever were to the East German secret police. As for Jutta, who shared my expenses and my pillow, I shall encounter her one day at a Bayreuth première on the arm of a cigar-smoking husband whom she dislikes just as heartily as she did the first, and who may also die in unfortunate circumstances.

Wish me luck.

All the best,

Harry (BA [with Honours], MCC [with Hope]).

A sun-terrace by the harbour
plus bottle of wine – evening
Kapsali
Kythira
Greece

April 22nd

Dear Janice,

The bad news first. The cultural soirée with the Greeks was not a success. The lady minister droned on so mellifluously about cradles of civilisation that her words acted as a lullaby and I fell asleep. Apparently I snored. This was not a good thing. The one person who appreciated my performance (not Piers, oh dear no!) was the Greek government minister with whom we went skiing a while ago. He detests the lady in question as he confided to me later (though she's remarkably like his wife), and was convinced I'd struck a blow for political change. Can there ever have been a minister with portfolio snored out of office before? Afterwards – and this brings me to the good news – he reminded me about his house on Kythira; as a result, hey presto, here I am. For a week.

Alone! I promise you. Alone on an island. I love it. The minister assumed I'd want to take Piers – how old-fashioned. I didn't disabuse him, knowing he'd be on the next plane if I did. When I told Jean-Claude he threatened to turn up for the weekend bearing champagne and scented words, but I've decided to keep him at arm's length for a while. Anything closer and the Gallic magic gets to work, and before I know where I am I'm teetering on the edge of a precipice, longing to jump. I also found the perfect excuse for a diplomat: suppose the government minister decided to put in an appearance to inspect his property and caught the French embassy *in flagrante*. He saw the wisdom of that immediately: *l'amour* may be his expertise and valued above almost all else, but not above *l'honneur*. I find this an intriguing moral distinction; it's perfectly all right to screw a fellow diplomat's wife in your own embassy – which he did – but not in a house belonging to a government minister.

So, I'm by myself and it's wonderful. I flew here from Athens yesterday morning at sparrow's fart. A tiny plane, eighteen-seater, skimming the waves and following the coastline of the Peloponnese. It would have been even lovelier if the pilot hadn't been a novice – apparently Olympic Airways use this route as a training flight (only eighteen passengers to drown). From my seat I could only see the instructor, and every so often a hurried hand would reach over and pull something, and the plane would miss a cliff by inches. I said more prayers than I thought I knew.

Finally there we were, bouncing on to an airstrip scratched out of the rock and scrub. And as if a trainee pilot wasn't enough agony before breakfast, the runway ended just before the cliff-top with one of those portable Stop signs you see in traffic diversions. No one else seemed perturbed, I have to say. The aircraft was packed with Australian emigrants returning for a holiday. Bronzed men in T-shirts and bush hats spilt out over the tarmac to greet tearful grannies in peasant black. Then everyone broke into Greek and piled into taxis, homebound, trailing plumes of dust. The minister had arranged me a hire-car (probably the only one on the island), and I threw my suitcase into the back and drove off without a map, heading south, knowing that on a small island you can't go far wrong without swimming. I was filled with a delicious sense of truancy: that's the spell of islands, enchanting you into feeling you're out of touch with the world and correspondingly more in touch with yourself (a pure illusion, I suspect). I took left or right turns on whim, delighting in not having the least idea where I was. Tiny roads meandered between villages through a spider's web of stone walls marking out forgotten fields. I drove into one village behind the mail-van and watched as the postman handed out airmail letters. Whiskery men settled themselves in doorways to read about suburban life in Melbourne or Wagga Wagga. One old lady adjusted her glasses and began to read aloud, intoning gravely.

Again I thought of the power of letters – their letters, our letters – and how nothing transmits our quiet thoughts quite as clearly as these rough and bumbling words.

You see how far away I drift, sitting here watching the sun paint brushmarks on the sea, and my bottle of wine two-thirds empty. I'm lonely, and loneliness brings its own special pleasure. I seek companionship in little things around me I mightn't normally even notice; so I've become deeply attached to a white duck who flatfoots it along the road past my terrace and treats the bread I throw as an insult inviting loud protest. It prefers the open drain, then settles down smugly under a tamarisk tree.

It would have been good if you could have been here, though from your phonecall I fully understood. *Church* v. *River Mews* certainly makes great matters of state pale: talking of which, isn't it curious how Papandreou marrying his mistress has turned burlesque into banality? Before, everyone was saying, 'Good for the old man that he can still pull the birds.' Now they're saying, 'What on earth's she doing with that old fart?'

Tomorrow I shall pick up the threads of *Alas*. I've just got to the Moscow bit and my hot-and-heavy with the KGB boss, which Piers was convinced would turn into another Profumo Affair. It was the only time he actually threatened to leave me. It was deeply unwise of me, of course, but he *was* gorgeous and – like Jean-Claude – seemed to put a love affair on a separate planet which the material world couldn't touch. I never did know if it was my fault he disappeared; it was the nearest I've ever come to mourning. I still think of him and wonder where he might be. I dream sometimes that he'll turn up in my path one day as Soviet Ambassador in some godforsaken capital to which my behaviour has condemned both him and Piers. What an epitaph!

Piers, I notice, now takes a suspicious interest in your welfare. Ever since he learnt about our bet, I see him eyeing me while I read your letters. Silence has always been his weapon, and something is going on behind that receding hairline. The idea of you racing off all the men in the street turns him on immensely, and just once or twice he enquires, 'What's the count reached now?' He's always fancied you rotten, of course, and the crafty diplomat in him is probably trying to work out how he can become one of the ten without fearful retribution from me. I'm also intrigued to know what he finds to tell Harry, who he's forever writing to. I doubt if they discuss the weather.

So, it's two months before we meet. Wimbledon fortnight. I won't enquire *too* indiscreetly how your battle-plan is working out because I know you'll tell me; it was part of the bargain, after all. But two months must put a strain on your ingenuity, especially with 'Arold still in residence. In every other respect you clearly flourish; being a subversive suits you. And being without Harry suits you even more. Keep it up – sorry, that's *your* battle-cry.

No sign of Aphrodite on her island. I think she must have left. Only a party of Germans heavily into being topless. When they play beachball I wonder how they know which is the ball.

I shall consider a discreet entry into the brine tomorrow, hangover and jellyfish permitting.

Love as always,

Ruth.

Dearest Ruth,

Your letter from Aphrodite's Isle arrived the morning I left to put Shakespeare on the map.

Now it's my turn for the bad news. The bet is off, alas. I hardly know whether to laugh or cry. And I didn't founder on 'Arold's goat-cheese-and-dirty-socks breath, but on something I've had absolutely no previous experience of – male fidelity. In other words, one of those four-in-every-hundred husbands who are allegedly faithful to their wives is alive and well and living in River Mews – damn him.

But to tell you the story. My collision with this hermetically-sealed marriage came hot on the heels of No 6 being scratched off the list. Courtenay. To describe it as a walkover might suggest sexual athletics, which it most certainly was not. A pushover? Oh dear, there must be some unloaded word to define what took place. All right, we 'did it' – as the young say – before coffee during a meeting to coordinate our campaign against the Rev Hope. Like the good and moral man Courtenay is, he acted on the principle that if he did it quickly enough God mightn't notice. He should have a successful career in politics; he's already mastered that politician's trick: talk loud and fast and the electorate won't realise it's being screwed. No wonder his wife seeks solace in long novels. He didn't even remove his pants. It was like being fucked through a hole in the wall. I lay back and thought of Wimbledon.

Enough said. I drove to Stratford next day hardly full of the joys of spring, but at least I'd scratched another one off the list, and as far as I was concerned *The Church* v. *River Mews* had just lost its assistant prosecutor. Now I had Shakespeare to attend to and Bill the architect waiting for me at the Falstaff Hotel. Except that he wasn't. A telephone message explained that he'd been delayed 'on site' in Warwick and would be arriving tomorrow. Seeing as how he'd been planning this little intimate number for several months, this struck me as somewhat cavalier. However, on discreet enquiry I learnt that he'd booked a room next to mine, and forgave him. I had to admit that successful architects might occasionally have more pressing things to do with their time than seduction. So I had a good dinner, watched *Hill Street Blues* in my room, and went to bed. I lay there for a long while thinking what it might be like with Bill; he's an attractive man, attractive because of so many hints at what he might be. I've always rather fancied him, and he clearly me. But – to be totally honest with you – what occupied my thoughts most of all was how I could get him to tell me what it was like for him making love to someone Nina's shape. (If they were your Germans I imagine they'd play beachball.) What does a man do, presented with all that ballast? On top he'd drown, underneath he'd suffocate.

Then in the morning – that was the day before

yesterday – I put on my Janice-professional gear and went sketching. Didn't take the car, just walked along the river; bright warm day, me in jeans and shirt, shoulder-bag with sketchpad, folding camp-stool and stuff, the sun in my hair and feeling wonderful – young, as if I was a student again. I stopped and drew a swan here and there, willows along the riverbank, even the odd cow. Then I thought, this is absurd. I'm not Turner, this is not the nineteenth century; nobody's ever going to want to look at the Janice Blakemore Stratford Sketchbook in the Tate Gallery; and what the hell's a camera for? What matters is not me doing a Ruskin with nature, but whatever I make of it back in my studio. So I packed away my sketching things and shot everything and anything I thought might come in useful. And of course they were quite different things: no cows, swans, willows at all, but shapes of old posts, water patterns, footprints in the mud, tree bark, and so on. I had to go back into town at lunchtime and buy a whole lot more film. So Turner became Cartier-Bresson.

I kept thinking of my oil millionaires and what they might expect from me. Was it reasonable to assume they'd never read a word of Shakespeare in their lives and therefore I could do whatever I chose, so long as it looked like Olde England? Or might they belong to that terrifying species of American tycoon, which almost by the wayside has found time for a PhD from Harvard and has seen every production of *Coriolanus* since the war, except for the Moscow revival last year; in which case they would certainly not want Anne Hathaway's cottage with hollyhocks, nor the River Avon at sundown with ducks a-dabbling? I resolved to consult Bill that evening.

But Bill wasn't there. I got back to the hotel about drinks time, my shoulders and back aching, hair a mess, jeans muddy, feet blistered; and no, he'd not checked in, said the receptionist, but would I care to leave a message for when he did? It was the same man I'd asked the previous evening, and he gave me a knowing look as if to suggest that the Falstaff Hotel was a research institute for the study of assignations and I was the fifteenth mistress to be stood up that week. I refused a ticket for *Volpone* and took a long bath, feeling despondent.

As I was drying my hair the phone went. It was Bill. Fulsome apologies: he was still in Warwick. A minor crisis. He would be in Stratford tonight, but late. 'Have a good dinner and I'll see you for breakfast around 8.' I got the impression that Janice's Shakespearean murals were the last things to be occupying his mind, let alone any extra-mural activities. I was cross and wished I was at home.

Then I went out and found an Italian restaurant called Romeo's. The proprietor looked more like Caliban. An American couple blustered in after *Volpone*, he ragged, she domineering behind Dame Edna spectacles on silver chains. Her 'O Sole Mio' Italian made no impression on Caliban, so she changed tack and tried out her English on me. The burden of her message was how clever it was to have put on a Ben Jonson play, since she was convinced Jonson had written all Shakespeare's plays anyway, and here it was being acknowledged in the very home of the supposed bard. I pretended to be

Swedish and non-comprehending. I heard her whisper to her husband, 'You know who that is? It's Liv Ullmann.' He looked non-comprehending too. It was that sort of evening. I thought of you alone on Kythira with your bottle of wine by the sea, and wished I could have been with you.

Bill turned up at breakfast brisk with apologies. I'd scarcely seen him away from Nina, and there was a marked difference: less friendly, more a man of the world, and a world in which women are a decorative frill. He had the air of a man who's got a portable phone in his pocket and is waiting for it to ring.

I told him what I'd done so far (omitting all mention of the camera), and that I intended to take the car off today to sketch some obvious places that might come in useful. He didn't appear particularly interested and switched the conversation to his own heavy schedule, then made me feel privileged that he'd definitely be free for dinner, 'And we can really talk.' About what, I wondered? He didn't sound as though he'd be in any mood to reveal what it was like making love to Nina. The final put-down came when he enquired about Clive's school (women's work), but before I answered he'd glanced at his watch and departed with a corny, 'Have a good day.'

Sod him, I thought. I'd been planning to look absolutely stunning that evening, breathing seduction, but now I felt thoroughly sour and decided to be sloppy and indifferent. I did a whistle-stop tour of Warwickshire all day – got lots of photos and did the odd sketch – then came back and raided the mini-bar luxuriously before getting back into my tatty jeans and a paint-stained shirt.

Bill was looking suave and polished at the bar – until he noticed me. I could see him wondering if the *maitre d'* would let us into the restaurant with me looking like the cleaning lady. He kept trying to shield me from disapproving eyes as we were shown to our table. So I put on my best *Eastenders* accent. 'Posh 'ere, in'it?', I said loudly. Bill looked disconcerted, which got worse when I pretended the grissini were chopsticks and said, 'Whoops! Can't take me anywhere, can yer?', as they shattered into pieces. 'Would madam care for an aperitif?', asked a stuffed shirt, sweeping up the debris with one of those little brushes. 'Just like the 'airdressers. Dandruff,' I exclaimed. 'Aperi – wot? This gentleman's just tryin' t'get me tiddly, you know, so 'e can 'ave 'is wicked way,' I giggled raucously. Then I ordered a Margarita, knowing from the previous evening that they wouldn't know how to mix one.

'Shall I order the wine?', Bill asked grimly. 'I'd like Blue Nun,' I said. I was behaving *appallingly*. He should have answered 'Nonsense,' and ordered Meursault, which would have shut me up. Instead he just looked blank, so I then insisted on sausages and mash with Branston Pickle (in fact it was delicious). Bill had Dover Sole and we shared the house wine, which was disgusting. (They didn't have any Blue Nun.) Conversation flowed even less than the wine. By the time it came to the sweet I was feeling I'd got my own back. Round One to Bill. Round Two to Janice.

I hadn't reckoned on Round Three. I couldn't keep

up the charade, and started to laugh. Wasn't the wine awful, I said, and why didn't we have a good claret with our cheese? Bill looked surprised, then relieved. He peered at me, intrigued. He has rather beautiful eyes, and they crinkle at the corner when he smiles. I gazed into them until he looked away. In the silence I took his hand and said, 'Forgive me, but you have been a pig.' He nodded and kept hold of my hand. 'I know . . . and I'm sorry.' Then he laughed. 'If it's any satisfaction to you, that wine was the direst retribution a man ever suffered.' He turned my hand over and added, 'Lovely, elegant hands you have. Nina's are peasant hands.' Ah ha, I thought. Here we go. But then he added, 'I married her because of those hands. Competent and safe. I knew I could trust myself to them for ever.' He smiled and returned my hand as though it was an inconsequential piece of frippery.

I persisted. 'And have you gone on trusting yourself to her . . . exclusively?'

'Oh yes,' he replied. 'Of course.'

'You've never been tempted?', I asked, raising my napkin to hide the fact that I was undoing several shirtbuttons.

'Oh, certainly I have. Many times. I'm tempted by you. Who wouldn't be?'

I put on my here-I-am look, and said nothing. Conversation at the neighbouring tables had suddenly dipped as low as my neckline. There was a sort of throttled silence of men pretending not to look, and of wives pretending not to notice. The Spanish waiter was most attentive with the wine. Bill gave a blink as

though one of my nipples had speared him in the eye.
He gave his nose a cleansing blow on a handkerchief.

'But that's what fidelity means, isn't it?' he said
rather softly. 'Not giving into temptation.'

'Not ever?'

'Never.'

I could have hit him – for costing me my debenture
seat, and for being what Harry could never be.

And that was it. End of bed. End of bet. The final
irony was that when we left the restaurant my back was
so painful I could hardly straighten up. Bill was all
solicitous. 'Poor you,' he said. 'You should ask Nina to
help you. She's wonderful with backs. Aromatherapy.
She's trained. A healing touch. Ring her when you
get back.'

Maybe I shall.

There doesn't seem a lot of point giving you any
other news. Clive's in yet more trouble at school – over
cricket. I always thought it was a sport for gentlemen;
not in Clive's hands it isn't. I wonder if Harry was like
that at his age, and the habit of dirty tricks simply got
transferred from cricket to women. I received a letter
from him, by the way. Apparently he's going to be
back in London for quite a while. He even asked me to
the National Theatre to see the new Alan Ayckbourn. I
said no. I'd like to see it, but not with Harry. Whatever
would we talk about?

'Arold's 'ouse is sold, apparently. But that's of no
interest to me now. Anyway, it's probably the retired
bank manager.

Ouch, my back hurts. Letter-writing doesn't help.

Sorry to sound grouchy. Your little blonde Venus feels more like Widow Twanky.

So it's back to art and real life. I've almost forgotten what that is.

With love,

Janice.

May

27 Parliament Hill Mansions
Highgate Road
London NW5

May 9th

Dear Piers,

　　The flat is wonderful. I emerged with pink eyes from
Bolton Grove last Monday and threw my toothbrush and
other valuables into the Peugeot estate I've treated myself
to. Then came a problem I'm unused to as a pampered
foreign correspondent – no resident's parking permit.
Fortunately your caretaker at the Mansions recognised
me from the box and found me a space in the yard –
next to the dustbins. However, I have to pay in kind,
listening to his exegesis on Islamic fundamentalism and
what Mr Major ought to be doing about the Bradford
loonies. 'Are you married?', he asked me this morning.
'I was once,' I said. 'Ah, plenty of men like you in the
Mansions,' he went on. 'Expect you'll be bringing lots of
women back. They all do: MPs, bishops, Arab sheikhs.'
Then he gave me one of those George Cole looks. 'If you

ever need any addresses, just ask. No problem.' I might have been back in Dresden.

Now, why did I ever imagine that writing a book was just journalism writ large? Here am I, author of thousands of newspaper articles, heaven knows how many book reviews, TV commentaries, pieces to camera and so on; and can I concoct even a coherent first sentence? Can I, hell. I have a sweet editor, rather mumsy, who invites me to lunch. 'Of course you can do it,' she says. 'Take a day off and go for a walk in the Chilterns. The bluebells will be out and you'll find ideas will soon fall into shape.' So I did, yesterday. It pissed with rain. I lost my car keys and hit my head entering ye olde pub for lunch.

The landlord finished off my day. 'I know you,' he said, 'You're . . . hang on a minute, I never forget a face. Got it . . . You're that David Dimbledon.'

I always thought writer's block was supposed to set in around midway, page 150 or so, not at the beginning. I gaze endlessly at the view from your window, and count the trees. I even go into the bathroom and turn on the tap, thinking that since running water can help you pee it might also help you write. Ah well! Tomorrow. Tomorrow. Tomorrow it'll all start to happen. 'The first rumblings of a revolution in Eastern Europe could be detected in a harmless announcement in *Pravda* that Mikhail Gorbachev . . .' Not bad, is it? Unfortunately I just made that up. Supposing I made it all up. Perhaps I'm a closet Le Carré.

Janice said no to the theatre, so I took an old girlfriend who used to be rather attractive. She's now important in Sotheby's and I got the impression that her reserve price has come down. I'm sure this is a sexist remark, but there's something odd about a woman being an expert on Japanese toggles. It wasn't the greatest of evenings.

I also had to phone Janice about collecting some files and documents I need. After your comments my antennae were out for signs of melting frost. What I detected on the telephone was not so much a Cold War as a Cool Cease-fire. She was just back from a sketching trip, she said (all expenses paid!), for some murals she's doing for a couple of stinking-rich Americans, and yes I could come round but preferably after dark; in other words, H Blakemore is not to be seen in River Mews during daylight hours. At least that reduces the danger of running into Amanda.

It was strange to be walking down a street where I'd once lived, to a house which was once mine, and to wait on the doorstep for a wife who was also once mine. She was ages answering the bell. In my vanity I wondered if she might be sprucing herself up for my benefit: it turned out she'd been washing paint off her hands. She was wearing a jumper and tight jeans – very fetching. But they were clothes I'd never seen, and they made me feel this was a Janice I'd never seen. She just said, 'Hello,' which could have been worse, I suppose. Then she showed me into what was once my study. She'd turned it into her studio: I barely recognised it. All my stuff was packed away in a cupboard, and she left me to sort through it. Afterwards she did offer me a drink, and we talked about Clive – communication by proxy. I said I was planning to go and see him at his school; I haven't seen the kid in six months, and God knows hardly at all for a year before that. Janice thought it sounded a good idea. 'He misses you.' She put a bit of warmth into that – by proxy. 'And are *you* all right?', I asked. As if in answer the phone rang. It was a man, and she was laughing. She kept turning her back to me and speaking low so I shouldn't hear.

There was a glow about her when she came back, and I had the cheek to ask if he was a lover. 'A lover?', she said, amused. 'What would the neighbours say?' The note of mockery made me conscious of how sexual an animal she is: it was as if I'd never made love to her, and wanted to. I wasn't sure if I felt jealous or excited.

'And what *do* the neighbours say?', I asked. She looked surprised. 'About what?' 'Us. The break-up.' 'Oh, I don't know,' she said, 'We don't talk about it.'

Well, that was a new departure. In earlier times of hostility she'd hold elaborate councils of war with just about every woman within a radius of five miles; and they'd sit over home-baked scones and pick over my imperfections like rich bitches picking over grubby clothes at an Oxfam jumble sale.

'You'd better go, I think,' she said. 'I think so, too,' I answered, gathering up my stuff. Then I lingered just a second and said, 'You're looking lovely.' But it was as if she hadn't heard. As the door closed I heard the phone ring again.

In the car driving back I wondered about her life and what she does, living alone in that gossipy little street. I know she paints – successfully too. But what about the rest? Does she ever see Amanda, and what the hell does *she* say? And who else? Ruth of course would know all about that, I imagine, and maybe you too. All I do know is that she seemed a woman strangely younger in looks and older in years.

As to our bet – well, my hunch is that you're wrong, and that you'll find yourself alone in the pavilion for the Lord's Test Match next month, with me waving to you from the beer-and-braces stand. At least I shan't have to wear that blood-orange-and-vomit-coloured tie.

Tuesday

Two surprises. First, I've managed to start the book and am no longer convinced I have Altzheimer's Disease. Secondly, I've been short-listed for a gong – as News Reporter of the Year. ITN rang this morning to offer congratulations, with hopes that I get it.

I can't see how, myself. I've not stood ducking bullets in Beirut, nor braved the Chinese army in Tianamen Square, although I suppose side-stepping Russian tanks in Lithuania might be worth a Mentioned in Despatches. If I'd died, of course, it would be mine for the asking, so to speak. All my vanity wants it, naturally. Besides, it might oil my career. George S who got the same gong for his Falklands reports back in 1982 says offers tend to pour in, and if I fancied New York or Paris rather than Vilnius and Gdansk there'd be no problem and double the pay. Then I might even be able to afford Clive's future criminal career, for which he's now being expensively trained.

I must say, perspectives do change when the sun shines, and maybe I should now hand over my marriage to the War Graves Commission and get on with life. Meanwhile, there's apparently a grand presentation ceremony next month, DJ and all that (mothballs time), and I shall be receiving a deckle-edged invitation for myself and my lady in due course. I suppose it's conceivable Janice might like to come, for the sake of auld lang syne. A fragment of her might be proud of me, and we could show a united front in flicking bread pellets at the opposition, if in nothing else.

What chances of you being voted Diplomat of the Year? Ruth would enjoy snoring through the ceremony.

The flat is still splendid. Your CD player is a lifesaver; your caretaker less so. He's convinced I should devote an entire news bulletin to exposing his local Indian restaurant.

Did you know the drunken lady next door was a Miss World in the 1970s? She showed me photographs to prove it, then told me who she'd slept with to get it. A surprising list. I declined the offer of being added to it.

As ever,

Yours,

Harry.

Dear Janice,

What cruel luck to have stumbled upon an endangered species on your very doorstep; it has to be divine malice. I propose we set up a World not-so-Wildlife Fund to ensure Bill is preserved for posterity.

You know, up to now I've lost every single bet I've ever made, and I'd become convinced this would be another. As it is, you need to tell me what a faithful husband looks like, so I may avoid him should we chance to meet. I have to say that Nina doesn't sound the kind of woman to be faithful to – whereas you, my dear, most certainly are, which suggests that fidelity and infidelity have very little to do with reason, and probably a lot to do with self-preservation. I suspect the truth about your Bill is low libido dressed to look like high morality. At least that's what we should tell ourselves, then we're entitled to feel cross with him. May all his buildings fall down.

So, what are we going to find to write about now? I don't think I want to hear how often you mow the lawn, or about battles with the vicar – though Abandon Hope has a most splendid ring about it, like a seventeenth century pulpit-basher declaiming against the horrors under women's skirts. And on your side, well, you don't want to hear about Piers's piles or our beloved ambassador's car being stolen, do you? The truth is, only scandal really endures, and sex is so much the most interesting thing in life that it's a wonder we ever talk about anything else. I suppose the answer is, we don't much. Or not if we can help it. Piers, funnily enough, doesn't, which is why I often find him so boring. But then he likes being secretive. It gives him a sense of power. I do sometimes wonder what he finds to tell Harry in those endless letters he writes. When I ask him he just says, 'Harry's an old friend.' 'So what?', I reply. 'I like him,' he says. 'He's interesting.' It's a curious feeling that your 'ex' probably knows a good deal more about Piers's private life than I do. Harry at least doesn't have a private life; he just waves it around in public, taking time off occasionally to pretend he's got his finger on the world's pulse instead of on some woman's clitoris.

Why do you imagine I'm so horrible about Harry? Piers is forever asking me that question; he suggested recently it was because I was the only woman Harry had never made a pass at. That could be true, I suppose. I wonder why he hasn't. Do you think he's anti-semitic? I prefer to think it's because he's scared limp of me. I shall ask Piers.

Janice, my darling, we shall meet in a little over six weeks – that's all. It'll be a great joy. Piers, you may know, has had the affrontery to lend Harry our flat so he can write some turgid book on Eastern Europe which will be out of date by the time it's published, and since he'll have to leave out his principal occupation it will also be rather thin, I assume. Piers tried to placate me by assuring me that the bastard will vacate the place for our visit to London next month. 'I should bloody well think so,' I said, and reminded him in my most Victorian manner that I wasn't in the habit of running a home for distressed gentlefolk. Piers took the line that Harry wasn't particularly distressed and in fact seemed to be having a pretty good time. 'Exactly,' I said, 'which is why we need to have the place thoroughly fumigated, and to look under the bed.' Piers thought I was being unreasonable, to which I proudly agreed, and that shut him up. It's a technique I've learnt: to behave badly, then agree I'm behaving badly but in such a way as to suggest that any other behaviour would be inept. This so offends his philosophical training that he's lost for words and I begin to laugh, which exasperates him even more. 'You're impossible,' is about the best he can muster.

The week on Kythira was idyllic. The government minister didn't put in an appearance, mercifully, but only I suspect because the government is about to fall any minute, and to be tracked down with the news on a remote island with a foreign diplomat's wife may not be the smoothest way to leave high office. He did phone me, however, and enquired who I'd met as if this were Hampstead; and when I said, 'A white duck,' there was a long silence. A sense of humour is not international currency.

Actually I met lots of people, including an Australian couple who'd 'come home' and built themselves a ranch house straight out of a Castlemaine XXXX advert: he'd removed the corks from his bush hat, but that was all. He – Greg – was growing Chardonnay grapes from the Barossa valley – delicious wine, the best I've had in Greece – and of course he was already making more money than anyone on the island since Barbarossa raped the place in the sixteenth century. His ancient Greek mother (not Barbarossa's, Greg's) used to sit on the doorstep all in black except for a bright red Gucci scarf. Occasionally she'd finger it before returning her knotted fingers to her lap. She'd never left the island, Greg told me; and when he tried to tell her how big Australia was, and how far away, she just smiled. I liked Greg.

I'd have stayed longer if I could. *Alas* progressed mightily between bouts of Greg's wine and feeding the duck. One headache has been what to leave out. I don't believe Piers would actually divorce me, but so much that's fun to write about concerns things I've never told him, and would really prefer him not to know. The Robert Redford episode, for instance. And that little moment at the Vatican. But since I'll never be able to publish it until Sir Piers is out to grass I've decided to go ahead, indiscretions and all, and hope he doesn't get his hands on it. I'd thought of keeping it in a folder entitled 'Nature Notes', but then Piers would be certain to open it hoping to find accounts of wild cyclamen. So what would really put him off? 'Knitting patterns'? 'Jewish cookery'? I know: 'Letters from Mother'.

Mock not; this is a serious matter.

And so, let me tell you, is the matter of Jean-Claude. I assure you, Janice, there's nothing to match the ardour of a lover who's convinced you've been away with another man. I don't know what energy the man has left for matters of state; all I can say is that if President

Mitterand needs his ambassador in Athens to do more than keep a check on French wine imports, he can probably whistle for it. I begin to wish Jean-Claude would take a tip from your Bill and practise fidelity for a while, or that his wife's ailing relative would either recover or die so the two of us could at least share the burden of his passion. Piers now chairs some unnecessary committee which conveniently sits in the evenings and exhausts him almost as much as the French ambassador exhausts me – though Piers, poor fellow, is not rewarded with brandy and roses.

I'm trying to decide whether diplomats' wives are just like any other wives, or worse. I came back from Kythira straight into a gaggle of unavoidable hen parties. Leaving aside the fact that they were all dressed as if for a staff meeting at Benenden School, seldom have I listened to such a chorus of timid complaint. The traffic. The pollution. Servants. The air-conditioning. The entertainment allowance. Boarding-school fees. The price of cornflakes. You name it; they moaned about it. What do you suppose it is that makes women who bear only the lightest of burdens behave as though life were propelling them towards a nervous breakdown? I thought of Greg's mother on Kythira, whose life has been all burden, and she's serene. It's the privileged who yap and whinge. It seems to be a disease of our sex which thirty years of Women's Lib has found no cure for, and it makes me angry and ashamed. And then of course I start being outrageous. 'Can anyone confirm,' I said, 'that the Yugoslav cultural attaché has the largest cock in the diplomatic service?' Well, I can tell you that took their attention away from the price of cornflakes. The beige brigade formed a protective stockade behind their teacups. When I told Piers he laughed, and said he was only surprised I couldn't answer the question myself.

So, I shall receive no further bulletins from the front. How I shall miss them. But at least I shall see you soon. And please, now that you have less to occupy your mind, will you come and stay in our lovely shack in the hills? Piers and I are going there for the weekend tomorrow to try and remember that we are married.

With lots of love,

Ruth.

Dearest Ruth,

I need rabbinical opinion urgently: is our Nos 1–10 bet about husbands or houses? If the first, then it's still *off*, and I shall start lobbying the powers-that-be to halt the sale of Wimbledon coverage to Sky Television (no dishes allowed here, being a conservation area; only bent and twisted bits of metal are permitted to sully our roofs).

However, if it's the latter then it's *on*, and you're now entitled to a full unexpurgated account of the latest events in what Kevin has christened 'River Screws'. I was thinking of offering you as an hors d'oeuvre the riveting tale of a battle currently raging between Nos 5 and 6 about the height of the new wall between them, in the hope that you'd be so bored by it you'd slaver for what follows and award the judgment in my favour: I badly want those seats! But I shall play fair. So here goes.

The drive back from Stratford was so painful because of my back that I decided to follow up Bill's suggestion and phone Nina. Doctors having failed to cure my back for the past eleven years – it all began after Clive was born – I'm now pre-disposed to go for anything the medical profession pooh-poohs; so why not try aromatherapy, I thought? I had no idea what this might involve: the 'therapy' bit I could grasp, but 'aroma' was a beguiling mystery. A cure by delicious perfumes: what could be better – even if administered by Nina?

She answered the phone rather briskly, assuming I wanted to talk about the latest round of *The Church* v. *River Mews*. 'No, Nina, it's my back,' I said. 'Bill suggested you might be able to help. It's bloody agony. I walk like an old crone.'

'I'm just off to play tennis,' she announced, as if tennis were good works. 'Come round this afternoon.' It sounded like a summons. We agreed on 3 o'clock.

Her garden was a carpet of bluebells. I sniffed them thinking they might be part of the 'aroma', but bluebells don't smell. Nina answered the door in a matronly way, and by now I was wishing I hadn't come. She was looking horribly healthy from tennis, and wearing a no-nonsense woollen blouse which would have looked voluminous on Mike Tyson but Nina filled it out like a schooner under full rig.

'In here,' she said, and showed me into a small room I'd never noticed. There was nothing in it except a rug on the floor and a shelf laden with lotions and potions. I had no idea what I was expected to do, so I just stood there like a prisoner in a cell.

'Your back, you said.' I nodded and tried to indicate the place where it hurt – but that gave me such a stab of pain I cried out. Nina made a 'Hmm' noise, then, 'Right. Shirt off and lie flat on your tummy, on the rug.'

Oh God, I'd never thought about this. As you know, I never wear a bra and it was too warm for a vest. If Nina had been a proper doctor I probably wouldn't have cared a damn. But here was a neighbour and a sort of friend; we'd talked about intimate things, and somehow that made the idea of taking my clothes off terribly exposing. Besides, I felt sure she'd take one look at my breasts and think how inadequate they are compared to hers. Mind you, Sophia Loren would feel inadequate next to Nina. I turned my back and tried to slip on to the rug without her seeing. It was a pretty slick manoeuvre, except that Nina ruined it. 'Shoes off, too. I may need to give you a foot massage. Pressure points.' Now, a contortionist might have been able to remove her shoes lying flat on her stomach, but not Janice Blakemore. There was no avoiding it. I rolled over painfully and sat up. I tried not to notice if Nina was looking at me, but it was a bit chilly and I was horribly conscious that my nipples were sticking out like thimbles.

'Just lie with your arms by your head. Try and relax completely. Fix your mind on somewhere ideally peaceful. Imagine yourself to be there. Don't think about me at all. You may find yourself dropping off to sleep.'

Sleep! My back was already doing a sword-dance, the floor was hard as rock, my arms were numb, my breasts squeezed flat, and I was feeling about as relaxed as a torture victim.

I waited for the agony of being pummelled. Suddenly there was the sound of music. I hadn't noticed a tape-recorder in the room. I even recognised it: Delius. I've always thought of him as thin-blooded, but now it was the most caressing sound imaginable. '*Appalachia*, isn't it?', I asked bravely. 'Yes, but you shouldn't talk,' came the terse reply.

I lay reproved. Bloody tyrant.

There was the sound of bottles being opened, and gradually the room became sweetly scented. I could hear the slushing sound of oils being rubbed between Nina's hands. Then her hands touched my back – firm, reassuring hands, pressing rhythmically into my skin. The fingers sought out lumps and bumps under the flesh as though my body were corrugated. Instead of the idyllic scene Nina had recommended, I had a picture in my mind of a heavy car driving over 'sleeping policemen' – and I wanted to laugh.

I've never been hypnotised, but that was what it felt like. Floating. I was no longer in that bare room but weightless at sea, and those strong hands were guiding me, steering me. I was only my body – no mind at all. No thoughts; just sensations. Delicious sensations. I began to hear myself making little noises of pleasure, quite involuntarily, and I didn't want to suppress them – couldn't have done. Like the noises you sometimes hear yourself making in dreams, though – this was the extraordinary thing – it was more like having sex, making love half-asleep. Does that shock you? It was because I couldn't see those hands, see whose they were; they were just pure touch, hands that knew how to touch, and where. And the sensation grew and grew . I've no idea if she told me to roll over on to my back, but I did. My eyes were closed, and I didn't feel able to open them – it would have broken the spell. I remember reaching out for her hands and laying them on my breasts. No words. I didn't see anything, and I don't know if I unbuttoned her blouse or whether she did. But we were naked and lying together. Knowing hands wandered over me everywhere, and I wanted them to. There was no shame. It was like being carried by the tide, and trusting that tide. I can't describe it, and I've no idea how long we lay there. I know I drifted off to sleep, and when I woke up Nina was dressed and holding out a mug of coffee towards me. She was smiling. I began to cry; it was as if my whole body was crying.

Only when I'd calmed down enough to sip my coffee did I want to panic. Christ, I'm a lesbian, I thought, and it was as if Nina understood without my having uttered a word. 'It was good, wasn't it? Bodies,' she was saying, 'women understand women. And why not? It's natural enough.' 'What d'you think it means?', I asked a little fearfully. She laughed. 'Nothing. Nothing at all. Just pleasure. Not the only kind.' 'You mean you like both?', I asked. 'Of course,' she answered.

Then she said something that took me by surprise. 'I guarantee one thing; you'll enjoy men more now.'

And do you know, I went and spent that night with Kevin. Just phoned him up and asked. I think I needed reassurance – perhaps Nina might have been wrong. She wasn't. 'Yer a hot little number, ain't yer, darlin'?' Kevin said in the morning. 'I told you before, you should come an' live with me.' Then I found myself telling him what had happened. He looked thoughtful. 'Well, I dunno,' he said, frowning. 'People like you could put me out of business. Sexual discrimination, that's what it is. I'm goin' to phone Nina an tell 'er, next time I want to be part of the action. Little and large, that's what you two are. An 'andful and an armful. I can't wait.' 'You may have to,' I said. 'Bloody bitch,' he muttered. 'At least my girlfriends are straight.'

So now I'm doing a painting of the River Avon with willows and little Shakespeare swans. Ruth, I don't know what to make of all this, but please may I have a ruling on the matter of No 7 River Mews.

Let me ease up by telling you about other things. Harry came and took away some of his clobber. I gather Piers has lent him your flat. He seemed rather subdued, I thought. He was like someone I didn't know, and I found myself wondering what I might have thought of him if I really hadn't known him. The most handsome man I'd met in years – certainly. And deliciously dangerous. But as it was I knew too much and remembered too much, and that spoilt it. So I kept extremely cool, and we talked about our little beast of a son. Then the phone went: it was Bill about the Chelsea murals, but I pretended it was a lover and kept glancing at Harry's face. He was jealous, and that tickled me. I wonder what he'd do if he really knew. He'd either kill me or be my slave for ever, and I'd prefer neither. After he'd left I had a strange feeling we might one day be the best of friends, at a safe distance.

One more item. 'Janice as Flora' has begun. All very proper so far – garlands of flowers and an air of Pre-Raphaelite languor in the sunlight. But the toga-like thing I have to wear has tempting possibilities, if I can stop myself laughing as I unwind it. Really, those Academicians are ridiculous: the notion that this is art. You always said I should have been painted by Botticelli: well, now I am, except that he's called Ambrose Brown. A further touch of absurdity is provided by his loopy wife who yesterday brought in Rosicrucian tracts for me to read while I posed. I preserved an air of springtime innocence with difficulty.

The new occupant of 'Arold's 'ouse moves in next week. An actor, I'm told. The name sounded familiar, though of course that could be because he's a lone survivor from *Dad's Army*.

Finally, I have to tell you that my back is much better, thank you. You seem to have been lying on yours rather a lot.

With love as always,

Janice.

27 Parliament Hill Mansions
London NW5

May 16th

Dear Clive,

This is to wish you a very happy birthday, and my heartiest congratulations on your triumphs in cricket and athletics. It was sad the match was rained off last week and I couldn't see you in action, but one of your mates assured me that you're already top of both the bowling and batting averages, and that you've broken the school record for putting the shot and for the marathon – an unusual combination, I must say.

I'm immensely proud of you. We must go to Lord's

together during the summer holidays; there's just a possibility I may be a member of the MCC by then, and shall be able to take you into the pavilion. You'd enjoy that, wouldn't you? Perhaps one day you'll actually play there, and I shall be even more proud. I only played there once and got a duck.

I hope the new cricket bat is the one you wanted.

With lots of love,

Daddy.

May 16th

Clive darling,

Many many happy returns of the day, and I hope the music tapes arrived safely. It was The Gorillas you wanted, wasn't it?

I must say, it was rather tactless of your headmaster to ring up this morning, just before your birthday. As always I never understand what he's talking about, and I wonder if he does. I think it's time the man retired. He clearly knows even less about cricket than I do. If those bits of wood you call 'bails' keep falling off, it seems the obvious thing is to stick them on so they can't. What's wrong with that? Isn't this the age of superglue? Anyway, I told him as much, and that he was jolly lucky to have a boy at his school with so much initiative and common sense.

As for that cannon-ball you're supposed to throw (I suppose you're not allowed real guns), why if it's so darned heavy don't they provide you with a lighter one? I don't imagine the Charge of the Light Brigade would have ended in slaughter if the Turkish cannon-balls had dropped at their feet. And since you discovered that one of those lavatory-cistern floats was exactly the right size, how sensible of you to use it. With all these lightweight alloys around these days, what on earth is the point of going on using cumbersome lumps of iron? I sometimes think schools want to prepare their pupils for living in the nineteenth century.

The business of the long-distance run baffles me completely. What do you call it? A marathon? Well, as I told the headmaster, I know a bit about classical history, and it's perfectly obvious to me that if the Greek runner who brought the news of the Turkish defeat had been able to find a short-cut from Marathon to Athens, then he would have done so. My friend Ruth lives out there at the moment, as you know, so I shall ask her if the man's actual route is known. My bet is that he certainly wasn't expected to run a zigzag course across half the country. So why on earth should you?

Anyway, there we are. It's glorious weather, and I hope you're enjoying it. I'm having my portrait painted in a ridiculous sort of toga that keeps slipping off, which is rather embarrassing.

With all my love, darling, and I'll see you on Founder's Day next month. I look forward to that.

Mummy.

ATHENS 1100 HRS MAY 18
CABLE DESPATCH TO: BLAKEMORE
1 RIVER MEWS LONDON W4 UK
SAPPHIC RITES WITH AROMATIC MEGA-
BOOBS DISGRACEFULLY ACCEPTED STOP
RUTH

May 19th

Dear Janice,

I tried to phone a couple of times but you were obviously out. There's something I'd like to ask you – no pressure and no strings attached.

An invitation arrived yesterday for an awards ceremony at the Guildhall on the 15th of next month. It's for journalists and media people generally, and I've been nominated News Reporter of the Year. I probably won't get it, having spent most of the year reporting non-news, but I suppose it's quite an honour and I'd love it if you'd come. There's dinner, glitter and stuff thrown in, boring speeches and the like – media wanking in front of the cameras; and if you couldn't bear it I'd perfectly understand. Don't feel you need to decide straightaway, but perhaps you could let me know within the next couple of weeks. I'd be grateful. (All right, here's a little bit of pressure: you'd look gorgeous. I thought so the other evening when I came round.)

The book progresses under my publisher's lash. I have an August deadline: they want something to show at the Frankfurt Book Fair in October. Hope the painting goes well. I'm so enjoying being back in London.

Clive seems to be excelling all round for once. Long may it last.

Love,

Harry.

Dear Janice,

I've had no experience of lesbianism; it's been one of those things I've always meant to do and never found time for, like learning Italian or reading Proust. I did have a threesome once, but that hardly counts since I never knew the man's wife was in the bed until it was too late. I also confess to a certain ignorance; what does one actually *do*? It may be prejudice, but I can't imagine any adequate stand-in for the male penis. All the vibrators, dildoes and French ticklers in the world strike me as poor substitutes, however ingenious and amazingly designed they may be. When I look in sex-shop windows, I'm bemused. Why bother? Call me old-fashioned, as Dame Edna would say, but for once it seems to me the divine architect got it absolutely right.

Having said that, I may just be the victim of circumstance. Here in the cradle of civilisation I don't happen to know any sweet-scented lady therapist built like a ship's figure-head. Greek ladies are dumpy and smell of sweat, and my Judgment of Paris would have to be from our modest circle of diplomats' wives who no longer (thank the good Lord) invite me to their tea-and-cakes soirées, and who probably think cunnilingus is some kind of geranium.

So, my pocket Aphrodite, the bet is on again. I'm delighted: I was beginning to view the future with some gloom. Only two to go, and all major obstacles must be behind you now. Ambrose Botticelli Brown sounds too romantic to pose a problem, and as for your actor – well, actors are never more than the roles they play, and how often did even Laurence Olivier get offered a part as irresistible as this? No lines to learn. No rehearsing. No make-up or costumes. Only a one-act. Applause guaranteed. As for first-night nerves, I expect he's used to them by now, and it's not as if he'll be alone.

I think I probably sound envious. What I do envy you for is – London. One can hardly imagine Dr Johnson suggesting that whoever was tired of Athens was tired of life. To be tired of Athens is obligatory – a city of touts, gigolos, unfed cats and tourists being served revolting food. And now we have another ridiculous general election which may get rid of Papandreou but certainly not the pollution. On election days in Greece, by the way, no one's permitted to buy a drink, so they throw hand-grenades instead. It's very jolly, I assure you.

Thank God for our country shack. We go there every weekend now. I write and get drunk. Piers hunts for flowers and gets less drunk. Nero the goat has become a resident. Piers tries to milk it (it *is* a she), and last Sunday in revenge she chewed up a pile of diplomatic papers he'd brought with him. 'Cheaper than the embassy shredder,' I suggested. But my beloved husband isn't given to bouts of humour at such moments, and grimly prepared his speech to the ambassador – who, incidentally, we had to dinner the other night. Excruciating it was, too. I was tempted to round off the evening with another Jewish joke, but Piers saw the look in my eye and gave me a kick under the table. I was very well-behaved, and was rewarded with the *on dit* that the French ambassador is likely to be elevated to Washington. That'll be another reason for loathing Athens. I don't believe I could manage Washington for the weekend.

So, roll on Wimbledon fortnight. We'll be here a bit before that. Can I come and spend a whole day with you in River Mews? You know what I'd really like – to take a peek at your fallen angels. Couldn't you give a party and invite them all? If you're really thinking of selling and moving out, that would be the perfect moment for an announcement. I could do it for you: 'Gentlemen, how pleased I am to see you all here since you have one thing in common.' Kevin could then propose a toast. You might even care to invite Harry.

Alas has reached Damascus. I wonder if Piers still believes I used to go to Palmyra to see the desert in flower. He is being very sweet. I think our goat has softened him. He talks to it more than he talks to me. But then I don't need milking.

Enough for now. *Bonne chance.*

Love,

Ruth.

May 26th

Dearest Ruth,

I'm so happy, I shall tell you everything at once. (1) I have two more commissions. (2) All Hope is finally abandoned. (3) Flora is deflowered. (4) The actor in 'Arold's 'ouse is unmarried and looks exactly like the young Paul Newman. (5) My garden is almost as gorgeous as he is. Oh, and (6) I have a new tennis opponent – Kevin, believe it or not.

Now I shall calm down and tell you more slowly. I suppose you'll want to know about Ambrose and how Flora shed her petals, but I shall make you wait patiently and inform you first about the tennis.

Kevin rang to insist we celebrate the Rev Hope's defeat – a gesture of Faith and Charity, as he put it. In other words, a game of tennis. This seemed unlikely, but Kevin claims to have been a county junior champion and not to have played since. On court it was easier to believe the second than the first. He'd brought along a bimbo as ball-girl, claiming I was quite young enough to do my own bending and fetching, and in any case he'd enjoy gazing at my legs. He'd got himself up in a sun-shield, dark glasses and a sweat-shirt with 'University of Gomorrah' on the front, and 'Twin-towned with Sodom' on the back. Dr Angus's wife passed by, and a look of horror rose from the depths of her Scottish soul.

As for Kevin's tennis racquet, it could have doubled up as a shrimping net. He maintains it originally belonged to Suzanne Lenglen. 'I suppose you're going to tell me you had an affair with her too?', I asked. 'Shhh!', he said as he gestured to the bimbo for another ball. 'Not in front of the children.' The poor girl was standing around trying to look like a mannequin and puzzle out the relationship between us at the same time.

'Nothing like healthy exercise,' he went on, and served the first ball straight over the far netting into the street. 'Just a warm-up.' The second one bounced his side of the net before joining its predecessor in the road. 'Love fifteen,' I called out cheerfully. 'You wait,' Kevin growled. 'Balls, girl,' he yelled at the bimbo. She rolled one across the court. 'Silly bitch, keep it up. If I can, so can you.' She tittered and threw another ball as if she was trying not to slip over on the ice. Kevin gathered it on the fourth bounce, and bowed in appreciation. Then he surprised me by serving a clean ace. 'Net cord,' I called out. 'Lying bastard,' he bellowed. 'Fifteen all. Now it's all happening, darlin'.'

It did all happen. It was five games all and we were reduced to one ball. The others lay hidden in various front gardens or beside overgrown graves. The bimbo was despatched to Kevin's house for reinforcements and returned with golf balls. 'All balls are the same to you, sweetheart, aren't they,' he said, smacking her on the bum with his racquet. 'Never mind.' And he proceeded to serve with the last remaining one. A real wind-up effort it was, a leap like Boris Becker. And plumb in! I never saw it, but it caught the top edge of my racquet, cleared the netting and delivered a fatal karate chop on Amanda's oriental flowering tree, which immediately set off the alarm to the police station and brought Ah-man-dah out with a shriek.

'Sorry, darlin': I'll put it in a splint for yer – not something I normally 'ave to do,' Kevin called out. 'Meanwhile you can 'ave this.' And giving a bow to the imaginary royal box he threw Amanda his sun-shield. 'Now you can boast that you've slept with a famous film director.' I remembered, of course, that she once had.

'God, you were foul to her,' I said afterwards. In fact I did feel sorry for Amanda; first she'd lost my husband, and now her prized tree. 'Yeah, I was, wa'n I?', Kevin answered, pouring out enormous gin and tonics. 'Shameful, in'it? Trouble is, she's a pretentious cow, an' people who queen it ask to be pulled down. Not like you,' he added. 'You're far more wicked than Ah-man-dah, but you play the dizzy blonde when it suits yer, and everyone melts. Except me: I 'arden up.'

He's right. I do play the dizzy blonde. I have these ludicrous conversations with Clive's headmaster on the phone, and I play all injured innocence until in no time he's apologising, telling me how clever and charming Clive is, and inviting me to visit the school and have lunch with him.

Now, Ruth, the good news. Bill's got me two more murals to paint at *double the fee*! I can't believe it. I'm rich. I shall be famous – at least in Saudi Arabia – they're Arabs who have two monstrous great houses in Surrey which Bill's converting into gin-palaces. I may even buy a new car.

And . . . 'Arold's 'ouse! Have you heard of an American actor called Paul Bellamy? I had vaguely. Kevin says he's big on US television. Presumably he wants a London pad. Anyway, big on TV or not, he's *beautiful*, my God. He introduced himself in that disarming American way just as I was leaving the house yesterday morning. Within two minutes I'd cut my hair appointment and was offering him neighbourly coffee in the garden. 'Lovely little place you got here,' he said, like they all do. Then lots more polite stuff, followed by, 'Alone, are you?', which was much more promising. 'Oh, yes,' I answered in an insouciant manner. 'Me too,' he volunteered. That was the best news of all. 'Perhaps we could have dinner one evening?', he said. I counted three for politeness, crossed my legs and replied, 'That would be very pleasant. Thank you.' He suggested Tuesday. I counted only two this time. 'Yes, I think I could manage Tuesday,' I said.

Oh, roll on Tuesday. Ruth, don't you think I deserve an Adonis at last? Mind you, I'd better be careful: I married the last one. But who was it (Freud?) who said you learn everything that matters about someone in the first thirty seconds after you've met. Well . . . if that should happen to be true, then this is a bit special. I'm trying hard not to overstate it, but I'm more than a little fluttering. It would be an amazing piece of poetic justice if, to qualify for my Diploma in Male Studies, I should actually graduate with a real man in my life. (*And* debenture seats to boot!)

Meanwhile, let me tell you about a *less* real man in my life. Here follows the wretched downfall of a Royal Academician.

I'll set the scene for you. Ambrose is a quiet, gentle person. Rather fine-looking in a mimsy-whimsy way, and I suppose fifty-ish. Elegant, well-preserved, desperately well-mannered. Silky voice – probably from years of calming down his wife. She's absolutely barking, though he loves her in a despairing sort of way. They have a beautiful, languid son whom I'd lined up if all else failed.

His studio is an extension of the house at the back. Acres of northern light and all that, and a secret garden like a miniature set for *A Midsummer Night's Dream*. This was evidently where I was supposed to impersonate Flora, goddess of flowers. I already felt a total idiot and wished I hadn't agreed.

The first afternoon we sat in the sun while Ambrose regaled me with the golden dreams of an artist. It was like being dropped back into the nineteenth century. His hero is Rossetti (DG, not Christina). I said I thought all Rossetti's women took laudanum and died miserable deaths, and he looked nervous and assured me it wouldn't be like that. What mattered, he said, was 'the idyll', something the camera was too crude an instrument to catch; only art could capture the true experience of beauty. Frankly I wanted to throw up. I thought I'd better not mention Francis Bacon.

He discreetly left me to dress up in this virginal toga thing he insists I wear. Then he returned after a timid knock on the door to arrange the garlands of flowers he'd already prepared. By now I was convinced he was even more out-to-lunch than his wife. 'What happens to the idyll when the flowers fade?', I asked. He informed me that he had an order at the florist for every afternoon I came to pose. 'I imagine that makes me the Goddess Interflora,' I suggested. But there wasn't a flicker of a smile.

So, very soon there I was, standing in the sunshine in his secret garden – a couple of hours it must have been – feeling like someone abandoned after the Cannes Festival of Flowers. Thank God Nina had sorted out my back. I wondered what Ambrose would have thought if he knew what his little idyll had got up to on the therapist's rug next door. Well, it was a boring way to spend an afternoon, but pretty painless, and when the sun disappeared behind the laurel hedge he gave a sigh of contentment and left me to change back into my T-shirt and jeans.

We had several sessions like that. He never showed me what he was doing. He paid me, I should add, in cash – forty pounds a time – in a sealed envelope. And each day I took the flowers away with me. 'They must always be fresh,' he explained carefully. After a week my sitting-room looked like the Chelsea Flower Show on clearing-up day. The dustmen are convinced I have a rich lover. 'Gor, ma'am, I'd give yer more than flowers,' they say as they heave the lot into the masher.

I only saw Ambrose's wife once, the very first time, when she pressed mystical tracts into my hand. I got the feeling he told her not to appear again, which was a relief in view of what I had in mind. He did say that she often goes to meetings; apparently there's a Rosicrucian lodge, or coven or whatever it's called, locally.

During the third or fourth session there was a sudden downpour which halted the proceedings, though not before my toga thing became thoroughly soaked and, as I suspect, diaphanous or at least clinging to all the right bits. Ambrose went on working for a while as if he hadn't noticed the rain. Perhaps he hadn't. I had to call out, 'Excuse me . . .' There was no mirror to embarrass me, but his voice had a distinct quaver in it while he made tea as if his life depended on it. 'Sugar?' 'No thanks,' I said, trying to look as though I was sweetness itself without it.

With the rain beating down outside and me gently steaming inside, this seemed the moment to take the idyll a step further. 'Don't you ever paint nudes?', I enquired in my most disingenuous voice. His mouth gave a twitch like a squirrel. 'Well, yes and no,' he said falteringly. 'No, really . . . I did once.' And he hesitated. It was like asking a Catholic priest if he'd ever kissed a girl. 'Louisa' (that's his wife) 'didn't like it,' he added. 'Why?', I asked. He delayed replying by offering me another cup of tea. 'Titian did. Rembrandt. Renoir,' I went on, somewhat unnecessarily. Ambrose cleared his throat and explained how his wife was deeply religious and her faith forbade bodies to be displayed publicly. I remembered she always dressed like one of those Victorian ladies climbing the Matterhorn. 'Wouldn't you like to?', I asked hopefully. 'Perhaps,' he said, looking embarrassed. He drained an already empty tea cup, then busied himself with the crockery.

Before long the rain stopped. I resumed my pose, still feeling and looking distinctly moist. Soon the light began to fade, and so did my garlands of flowers. Ambrose retired politely while I prepared to remove my vestal virgin outfit. I was getting quite good at it by now: I treated it like a large lavatory roll and wound it round myself, beginning at the thighs and bringing a final loop fetchingly up over my bare shoulders. I had to be careful the folds overlapped or I looked like a Venetian blind on legs.

'I like you so much,' Ambrose said, as he held open the front door. He'd quite recovered his composure since my enquiry about nudes, and was smiling broadly. 'I shall be sad when it's done,' he added. 'One more session; that's all I'll need. Then I'll show you the picture. It's changing quite a lot.' He didn't explain.

The next afternoon I duly wound myself into my outfit for the last time. But he had a surprise for me, he said. A bright idea. 'Look, I've picked these. I've decided I want to paint you holding them.' And he handed me a bunch of lilac.

Now, I don't know if you remember that weekend we had in Dorset once – the four of us, years ago – Piers rented a cottage. It was just before you both went off to Russia. It was lilac season, and I spent the entire weekend with my nose inside a box of tissues.

Well, *you* may remember, but when Ambrose handed me that bunch of lilac *I* didn't. And now I'll tell you what happened to your sweet goddess of flowers and Ambrose's gentle Pre-Raphaelite idyll. I posed with my lilac. And then it began. First a tickle in the nose. Then a sneeze. Then another and another. No ordinary sneezes – volcanic eruptions. I was helpless. The maestro put down his brushes and hurried over with a handkerchief and a consoling arm. And at that moment, an extra-special-multiple sneeze engulfed my whole body and in doing so shook my toga thing clean off my shoulders. Not just my shoulders: it began to unwind itself like one of those tennis balls attached to a pole with elastic, until in no time it had subsided in a heap at my feet, along with the lilac. I was left clutching Ambrose's handkerchief with one hand and my modesty with the other – starkers except for my panties.

For a moment we both just stood there – sheer suspension of belief. At first Ambrose tried not to look, then pretended not to look, then stopped pretending – until I dropped my handkerchief along with my modesty. 'Does this count as displaying my body publicly?', I asked. He gave out a sort of soft moan, which I interpreted as surrender. The grass was a bit damp, but so was I, and before long it was just as well that Louisa's prayer meeting didn't break up early.

There was one final surprise. When we were respectable again, Ambrose kept his promise and showed me the painting. There was no lilac in it, of course; otherwise it was all but complete. It was certainly a most faithful portrait of me, even down to the birthmark on my left breast. It was a portrait of me entirely naked!

So much for idylls.

'I'm afraid it was your question about nudes which put me in mind of it,' he said, a little shyly.

'What? The painting, or making love?'

'Both, I regret to say.'

'I see,' I said. 'But tell me please, how did you know what I look like before . . . ?', and I did a sort of mime of the unwinding process.

'My lovely lady,' he said earnestly, 'I'm sure I'm not the first to tell you how exactly you resemble a Botticelli Venus. And after all, I'm an artist, and I do know my Botticelli.'

'And the birthmark?'

He didn't answer, and I left.

There are just two remaining questions. Will he dare show it to Louisa? More important, who else will he show it to? I don't greatly care to hang, naked as nature intended, in next year's Royal Academy Summer Exhibition. What would the neighbours say? All right – I know.

Finally, let me switch to a matter concerning Harry. He's been nominated for a grand award and is begging me to go with him to the ceremony. I'm torn. There's no anger any more; but neither do I feel like his wife any more, and I don't fancy spending an evening having to pretend I still am. But he was humble and sweet about it, and considerate – all the things he usually isn't – and there's a small voice inside me which says, 'Go.' I *would* be proud of him if he won – to know that there is something he is really good at, even if it isn't marriage. If only it could have been the other way round; I would never have minded him not being successful if he could have been successful with me.

There's another small voice inside me, too. It says, 'What will you feel watching Harry on the box looking magnificent in his DJ, and sitting next to him is some edible model of twenty-two squeezing his thigh and planting kisses of congratulation on his cheek?'

It's not jealousy, it's pride. I'm almost thirty-six, and Harry's forty. Unfair, isn't it?

Yes, I *am* jealous.

Until Wimbledon, then – with lots of love from the Goddess Interflora,

Janice.

> *27 Parliament Hill Mansions*
> *Highgate Rd*
> *London NW5*
>
> *May 28th*

Dear Headmaster,

You leave me no choice in the matter. Of course you were entirely within your rights to act as you did, just as I am entirely within mine to express an opinion about your school and the way you choose to run it.

In my experience, a school is as good as its ability to channel the energies of difficult children; or, to put it another way, a school is as bad as its worst children. If Clive's record of behaviour is 'verging on the criminal', as you delicately put it, then perhaps your establishment might more suitably offer itself as a preparatory school for Wormwood Scrubs; at least the fees would then be considerably lower. And in view of your own past convictions for 'embezzlement and misappropriation of corporate funds' (*The Times* law report, October 24th,

1964), I can imagine no one better qualified to be in charge of it. With such personal experience of the criminal mind, it remains a mystery to me how you should have failed so lamentably with Clive. But perhaps great skills fade with advancing years, and we should not look beyond that all-too-familiar ogre of our time – the generation gap.

I note that you are prepared to keep Clive at school until the end of this present summer term. I am sure this generosity is untinged by any wish to add the England Junior Schools Cricket Cup to the other trophies so proudly on display in your Great Hall.

I remain, yours sincerely,

Harry S Blakemore.

Dear Piers,

One penalty of living 'on site' is having to referee those interminable domestic squabbles that make the world go round. Janice, as a hard-working 'professional', has taken to re-directing all such matters straight to Parliament Hill Mansions, no doubt to counter-balance those many years when H Blakemore was incommunicado in Warsaw or Leipzig. Memos sometimes get attached: 'Harry, for your attention', or, 'Harry, action, please'. Little minx.

In short, Clive's being expelled at the end of this term. I followed a tip-off about the headmaster's past and discovered that he did indeed have a criminal record and had since changed his name. My letter pointing this out will have caused him a great deal more discomfort than was suffered by the boy Clive is supposed to have wounded in the school production of *Macbeth*. They should have known better than to give my enterprising son lines like, 'Is this a dagger which I see before me?' So, it's back on the school safari once again. But who wants a delinquent boy of twelve? Maybe it's not too late to put him down for Borstal.

The deckle-edged invitation duly arrived, but no answer yet from madam as to whether she'll deign to accompany me. At least she didn't fire off a 'FO' telegram like the last time I made overtures; so if silence is indeed golden I may still find myself next to Janice at the Guildhall watching some *Panorama* creep receive the award I don't deserve.

What irks me is that I wouldn't be going through any of this born-again-Romeo performance were it not for your tantalising bet and your persistent view that Janice is lying awake at night longing for my return. You've said as much so many times now, in spite of my evidence to the contrary. I thought it was a journalist's privilege never to reveal his sources, while diplomats were simply supposed to travel the world lying for their country. Your source – though you decline to acknowledge it – has to be Ruth and her little hotline with madam. But since Ruth can't stand me, and neither as far as I'm able to tell can Janice, it's hard to imagine honeyed words passing between them. Which leaves you with a rather suspect gift of second sight. I think actually our bet ought to be the other way round: that as a reward for my fruitless and humiliating labours you fix me membership of Lord's when I *fail*. Will you kindly consider this counter-proposal?

The book progresses. The first couple of chapters have gone off to my editor, who seems surprised that a journalist can actually write English – which I find mildly insulting since most of her bestselling hacks can't. She's taken to inviting me to publishers' parties – incestuous occasions full of authors trying to be recognised and their mistresses trying not to be.

I've also met – definitely *not* at a publishers' party – quite the most voluptuously beautiful and entirely vacuous girl ever born. She would make any Page

Three girl appear over-endowed with brains and under-endowed in other departments. To be seen out with her is the most terrific ego-boost imaginable: it's astonishing the number of men who discover the need to talk to me, though I'm toying with the idea of telling people she's a deaf-mute so I don't have to listen to her answer '*Reelly*' when they try to chat her up. Your Joyce Grenfell secretary may be no Helen of Troy but I bet she doesn't think *glasnost* is a pop group. I take her to quiet restaurants and pretend she's a work of art; one doesn't expect to hold conversations with the Venus of Urbino. When we make love I daren't murmur a word in case she says '*Reelly*'.

Your caretaker, though, thinks I've got admirable taste. He's taken to finding me a parking space further away from the dustbins.

And how did the general election go? Does the end of Pasok mean anything at all beyond new hands dipping in the till? A month's bashing at my word processor and I'm already itching to be out in the market-place again. Being an author is like always re-heating yesterday's dinner. But I think I'd like a change of scenery; I've had enough of life painted grey. Cross your fingers for me at the awards ceremony – June 15th, incidentally, a week or so before your arrival. I'll have de-camped by then, of course; a TV producer friend is lending me a room for the time you're here, and it's not – thank God – underground.

From then on, it's deadlines forever. They want to rush the book out for Christmas. Where I'll be by then, heaven knows. ITN are making noises about the Far East. That at least would be far enough from River

Mews and the grave of my marriage. Hong Kong in its last years of grace might be fascinating, and I have old friends there.

Meanwhile, it'll be good seeing you again – *reelly*!

All the best,

Yours,

Harry.

June

June 2nd

Dear Janice,

Summer has arrived on a magic carpet of fumes. Jean-Claude assures me that EC subsidies take the form of sending to Greece all the lead no longer put in petrol elsewhere in the Common Market. By the time we return from England he'll be Mitterand's man in Washington, alas. Or *Alas*. Another chapter over. He promises visits, but French promises may be about as enduring as French kisses. We plan a farewell weekend at the Chateau Le Corb – a last look at the wine-dark sea, and a last embrace in the fountain of tears. How ludicrous I make it sound: how ludicrous, maybe, it is. My life entirely lacks all those commitments one is supposed to make as proof of being a serious woman. Thank God yours does, too. It's humour and sex that make the world go round; if we were all poll-tax marchers we'd suffocate in a Brave New World. I like the Cowardly Old World too much. I'm a sentimentalist at heart: I love our country shack and the raw hills, the sound of sheep-bells and the ricketty table where I sit and read, or write *Alas*. Perhaps this is my real *Wonderland* after all the Jean-Claudes have left to rule the world. Or am I just preparing for middle age?

It was my birthday yesterday – a hateful month when I'm a year older than you.

I cross my fingers for you with Paul Newman Jnr. But be careful with beautiful Americans; I've met too many who are Snoopy dressed as Prince Charming.

Piers' letters to Harry seem to get longer and longer. Do men write to one another about the same things women do? 'How would I know?', Piers says smugly. 'Of course you bloody well do,' I answer. 'You read mine.'

He's getting very lustful these days. His piles must be better.

Love as always,

Ruth.

PS I don't imagine there'll be a chance to write again before we leave. So, all rests on Paul Newman. I cross my fingers for you, and your debenture tickets are safely wedged between them. See you in River Mews. But please, no aromatherapy for me – just in case you had it in mind. I'm an orthodox girl; remember, I'm Jewish.

Dearest Ruth,

I shall tell you the story of Tuesday's girl – exactly as it was – no trimmings, and nothing trimmed.

It was *that* Tuesday, the one I told you about. Here I was, almost thirty-six, feeling sixteen, daydreaming about my dinner date with a movie star. Romance never seems to grow up: I was in a state of nerves for days, no work done, broken nights, broken crockery, forgot to feed the cat. Kevin took one look and said, 'Oh Gawd' and left. Then he sent a good luck card with the words, 'If it's thumbs down, come to Paris for the weekend.' I'd see Paul pass by along the street in his Bloomingdale suede jacket cut to show off his torso, and his trousers cut to show off his manhood; and I prayed he wouldn't get trapped by some other bitch while he was out. I wanted to lock him up until Tuesday, then handcuff him.

The day arrived. He phoned early. I was convinced he was going to call it off, and could hardly speak. The voice was black velvet. 'Janice, is it still fine with you?' Oh boy, was it still fine with me! I tried to say calmly, 'Yes, absolutely,' but it came out in a squeak. He laughed. 'Are you OK?' I gulped, 'Yes'. 'Would 8 o'clock suit you? I'll call a little before. I've ordered a cab. I'm looking forward to it.' 'Me too,' I said feebly.

I did nothing all day but get ready and unready. I had my hair done by Timothy. Lay in the bath. Did my nails. Wandered round the house glancing at my watch and pulling out dresses which I put away again. I rearranged the flowers, plumped up the cushions, freshened the pot-pourri, put out cheese biscuits and threw them away because they were stale. Then I searched for an ashtray; did he smoke? What did he drink? What *did* American actors drink? Probably some cocktail I've never heard of. The room suddenly looked so awful I pulled the furniture around until it looked worse. By that time I was sweaty and needed another bath. I kept looking in the mirror, and each time my crow's feet had grown half an inch. By 7 o'clock I was beginning to panic, and I'd still forgotten to feed the cat. 'Pull yourself together, Janice,' I ordered, and settled for my Jean Muir dress – the clingy look – others in the street may have seen it, but not Paul. I hoped he didn't prefer women with enormous boobs; at least this dress made the most of what I've got. Finally the Giorgio; I put the bottle aside until I actually saw him leave No 3 so the perfume wouldn't fade. At that moment bloody Amanda drove past and stopped. Wound down the window. I could have kicked her arse. She had her violin in the back seat, and I could see Paul asking polite questions. She was smiling and wriggling like a spaniel, tossing her hair. 'For fuck's sake take your fiddle and piss off, Amanda,' I wanted to shout.

Then the taxi drew up, which halted the cosy little duet, mercifully. I say 'taxi': it was a chauffeur-driven white Mercedes. At last Amanda drove off, hitting the curb. Good! I dabbed on more Giorgio and hurried into the kitchen so as not to open the door the moment Paul rang the bell. A final glance in the mirror. To hell with the crow's feet: I looked terrific. I felt awful.

Paul was wearing a silver-grey suit which showed off the sun-tan and picked up the flecks of grey curling above his ears. I guessed him to be around forty. I found myself wondering how many ex-wives he paid alimony to, and felt ashamed at the thought. For Christ's sake, I'd met this guy *once*; what was I doing speculating? Here was a man who probably had a mistress at every airport. Never mind: for this evening at least he was mine.

He accepted a vodka and tonic. I'd bought a lime specially, and dropped in a slice of it as he took the glass. I saw him look at my hand: no wedding ring. I glanced at his: none either. But then men generally don't. He admired the room, looked at the books, ('You read Updike') and the CDs ('Bruckner – my God!'); actually it's Harry's, I can't bear Bruckner. Then it was time. The chauffeur saw us leave the house and hurried to open the rear doors. I wondered who was watching, and didn't dare look. 'There's a restaurant I like to go to when I'm in London – I hope you like it,' he said. 'Small. Quiet. No Bruckner,' he smiled, 'I hope you don't mind. Italian. Pity it isn't the white truffle season.' White truffles were the last things on my mind. I liked his profile, I liked the smell of him, and the laughter lines round his mouth.

It was broad daylight, but the restaurant was dark. Low candles. Fresh flowers. Vivaldi in the background. Operatic singing and the smell of herbs from the kitchen. Paul called the waiter Nando. He ordered champagne ('I hope that's all right with you'). There were eight or nine other tables. Only one of them was occupied some distance away; a man and a young woman, both too absorbed to notice we'd come in. I caught a glimpse of her and was glad Paul didn't seem to have done: there was so much bosom exposed I wondered where she kept her nipples.

I thought of you and Jean-Claude, and what you said about the art of love being to take you travelling with him wherever the conversation went. He'd filmed with Brando, liked working with Coppola, despised American TV, but soaps made him a packet and gave him the lifestyle he likes. He ordered more champagne as if it was the house wine, and I hoped he'd take my hand. He could have kept it. Never mind – we had the whole evening, the whole night, and all those tomorrows. I told him about my murals and he said he had to have one. 'What of, do you think?', I asked. He laughed.'Maybe a desert. Are you any good at deserts?' 'Just sand, isn't it?', I said. 'And space,' he added.'Lots of it. That's what I like.'

It must have been the mention of 'space' that did it. Probably I should have noticed before how he kept gazing across the restaurant. I tried to believe he was picturing the glamorous places we'd been talking about, with me looking stunning in the centre of each picture. I already had the most seductive desert imaginable in my mind for his mural. But gradually it dawned on me that it might not be me he was dreaming about for his desert. His eyes kept switching to the same place across the room. I dropped my napkin in order to have a good look. The glamorous creature at the far table was leaning forwards, holding the man's hands and practically serving her breasts on his plate. Nando the waiter was pretending not to look. Paul was *not* pretending; he was looking. I wanted to go over and tip my champagne down her Grand Canyon.

'Quite a figure,' I said archly. Paul looked at me, puzzled. 'Who?' 'The girl over there.' He still looked puzzled. 'I hadn't noticed her,' he said. Lying bastard, I thought.

The conversation had gone flat. We had our sorbet in silence. I was beginning to feel miserable. What hope had I got if the mere sight of a pair of knockers was enough to distract the man of my dreams? He was just as bad as Harry.

Then the couple rose to leave, and my stomach went into a knot. I hadn't been paying any attention to the man. It *was* Harry!

As he passed our table he saw me and stopped dead. Tits-bum-and-oops-a-daisy crashed into him (must have been like being mugged by two tons of marshmallow) and started giggling, 'Ooh 'Arry, reelly!'

Before I had a chance to be coolly dismissive Paul was on his feet, all New World charm and firm hand-shake. 'Hi, I'm Paul Bellamy. Won't you join us for coffee?' There's a special look Harry gets when he's furious and knows he hasn't got a leg to stand on. Well, that was how he looked. 'Thank you, we'd love to,' he said (what else could the poor bugger say?). And he yanked Streaked Blondie next to Paul where she sat wobbling while he sat himself next to me.

Harry opened the hostilities. 'Have you ever seen anything more vulgar than that stretched white Merc outside? Some old has-been's tart-catcher, I expect.'

Paul just laughed. 'Guilty, I'm afraid. I haven't

got to grips with this English business of mini-cabs. I imagined they'd all be small so I asked for the largest cab they had.' He smiled so sweetly, my heart did a somersault and Streaked Blondie wriggled in her seat as though something was getting very hot. 'Let me try and recover some honour by offering you a truly fine brandy.'

Nando came over at the wave of a hand, and Harry and Paul slipped into one of those tedious conversations about the respective merits of two brandies which I knew would taste exactly the same.

Blondie then distinguished herself. ''Scuse me, I 'ate brandy. Can I 'ave a *creme de menthe frappé* . . . wiv a straw?' In the silence that followed she went on, 'I went to Marbella last year. They give it to you wiv one of them little parasols on. Reelly nice.' And she smiled at us benignly. I nodded, 'Nothing like a little parasol, I always say.' Paul looked uncertain, Harry sharp. Blondie said, 'Yeah. Reelly nice,' and treated Paul to a five hundred megawatt smile with added boob wobble.

Surprisingly, Paul looked away and turned to Harry. 'I saw your reports from Lithuania when I was over here last. Impressive.' Harry preened modestly – the cool upright Brit. 'Just job-lotting.' Paul insisted, 'Oh no, not at all. Put me in front of a camera and I'm dumb until someone gives me some lines. Someone who can think on his feet while tanks are rolling over people . . . well!' He shook his head in admiration. 'You were in Romania too, weren't you?' he added. 'I'm going there next month. Making a programme to raise money for those orphanages.'

Next minute he and Harry were deep in conversation about Eastern Europe, and Streaked Blondie and I were marginalised.

I was becoming decidedly confused. Next to Harry, Paul was looking a touch plastic. You know that look when everything's just a bit too studied. I was also aware that Paul was considerably more animated than he'd been with me all evening. His eyes were shining and his face hadn't left Harry's since they'd sat down. I don't know if it dawned on me slowly or not, but it certainly dawned on me: my prince was a poof – Albertine, not Albert.

I suppose I should have been devastated. All that effort and excitement, and the debenture seats lost in a low blow to the genes. But suddenly it seemed hysterically funny. There was Harry, as territorial as a silver-backed gorilla, thinking wifey was being trespassed on; SB like a four-year-old let loose in a sweet shop with two delicious men and only a skinny housewife for competition; and all the time Paul hot for Harry. The combination of all that, plus champagne, plus brandy, undid me and I started giggling. Then I thought of your face when I told you, and that made me giggle even more until I couldn't stop. I managed to splutter to Paul, 'I do think it's irresponsible of you to be wining and dining gullible women. It gives the wrong impression, you know.' Then the giggles took over again.

Harry leapt to quite the wrong conclusion, hauled me to my feet and said, 'I'd better take my wife home.' Paul and Blondie looked as though they'd been slapped with a wet kipper. 'Your wife!', they both squeaked, as Harry pulled me out of the restaurant, Nando moaning

'Mamma Mia,' and me struggling to stay upright. Harry poured me into the back of a cab, jumped in himself, and then lectured me all the way home, ending with, 'If you don't care what I think, what about Clive?' Well . . . the thought of Clive – Clive as my moral guardian – finished me off. I was sobbing with laughter by the time we got to No 1. I could barely get the key in the door, though I did manage to shut it on Harry. Then I collapsed into bed and laughed/cried myself to sleep.

Next morning hundreds of gnomes were using road-drills inside my head. I was sick twice, and miserable about our bet.

Later I thought perhaps if I told Paul the whole story he might be able to do it just once with his eyes closed. Or perhaps you might accept the bet as won if Harry did No 3 for me instead. Unlikely, I know.

So you may uncross your fingers; your tickets are safe. This time there'll be no last-minute saviour. I've met my match. Aphrodite intends to retire and tend her roses. At least they have pricks I can kick against.

Love in the deepest despond – but may I at least share your strawberries at Wimbledon?

Janice.

June 12th

Dear Piers,

Thanks for letting me know the date of Ruth's arrival. I'll make sure I'm well out of the way, and the flat spotless. My address while you're here, by the way, is 35a Curzon Road, W9 – inconveniently close to Lord's for someone who's most unlikely to be joining you in the pavilion for the first Test Match, and who can't see himself queuing for tickets at dawn behind two thousand West Indians blowing trumpets and practising break-dancing.

This growing pessimism springs from an unhappy incident the other evening. I'd just received a note from Janice agreeing to come to the awards ceremony next week. I was so pleased I decided to treat myself to a little celebration, in the form of inviting 'Reelly' to a candlelit tête-à-tête in the Highgate restaurant we go to sometimes when I feel in the mood for contemplating the good things in life. The fact that another couple took a table across the room didn't matter in the least, of course: what did matter was that the woman was Janice.

From that moment things began to go wrong. Janice was with some smooth operator who was plying her with champagne and sweet-talk by the bucketful. Each time I glanced in her direction she seemed even more like a rabbit dazzled in the headlights. I became furiously indignant: how dare my wife allow herself to be seduced by this rich creep? I wanted to do a Kirk Douglas and sock him on the jaw. But not being alone I couldn't do a thing, especially as Reelly's dress and what escaped from it hardly suggested that she was a nice girl on her way to Evensong. What made it worse was that Janice was looking absolutely stunning, and I would so much rather have been with her than with my piece of naked upholstery, who'd been informing me all evening about the new Sidcup Shopping Precinct.

Eventually I decided it was time to run the gauntlet. No such luck. We were waylaid. Smoothy-pants wanted to spread his charm around. Brandy flowed. Reelly recognised the guy to be an American actor and laid out her goods for tit-inspection. Janice was by now pissed out of her mind. Then I lost my cool, abandoned Reelly to her familiar fate and swept Janice off magnificently in a taxi. Sir Galahad to perfection.

It was *not* a success. Chivalrous knights don't expect to be mocked, least of all to have the front door slammed in their faces. The real humiliation came the following morning. I rang a friend who's in on showbiz. 'Paul Bellamy,' he said, laughing. 'That famous faggot. Matey, it was *you* he fancied!'

Through all the mortification, I've come to realise you may well be right about Janice after all; that she's leading a fairly quiet and celibate life, choosing men guaranteed not to leap on top of her. But then she was always a bit like that; sex has never been something she found particularly easy to cope with. Whatever, I fear there'll be a heavy ground frost at the Guildhall next week. I'm beginning to wish I was back in Lithuania.

So, you're coming over on the 23rd. I shan't pinch your MCC tie when I leave the flat. Ruth will presumably be lost to Wimbledon for the forthcoming fortnight, much to Janice's envy, while you'll be hobnobbing with the geriatrics in the Long Room at Lord's, much to my envy. I shall watch it on telly, and feel smug when it rains.

I'll ring. We must have an undiplomatic dinner or two. I look forward to that.

All the best,

Harry.

LONDON W4 1000 HRS JUNE 14
CABLE DESPATCH TO: CLIVE BLAKEMORE
WILLIRISING SCHOOL CERNE ABBAS
DORSET
HUGEST CONGRATULATIONS MAJOR
SCHOLARSHIP PAGANINI SCHOOL STOP
NEVER KNEW YOU PLAYED VIOLIN STOP
ALL LOVE
MUMMY

(In Greek) Communication
damaged in transit

27 Parliament Hill Mansions

June 17th

if it was foresight or guesswork on your
cunning sod; none the less it's happened.
lutions all round Eastern Europe I've
here: in short, Janice and I are
fully when we meet – in the Lord's pav-
have to thank first of all the gentle-
day before yesterday voted me News
esumably for my sharply-honed skills
senting non-news as news. Ladbroke's
tsider's odds; and feeling diminished
Beirut and Ethiopia veterans complacent
n rather too liquid style. In consequence I
Lunchtime O'Booze Award was mine until Janice
elbow into my ribs, and before I knew
blinking into cameras and micro-
shaking hands with heaven-knows-who.
speech apparently flowed from elsewhere,
f thanking everyone under the sun from my
cleaning lady, including, 'My beloved wife
tting up with me or not as the case may be.'

aughter before I even knew what I'd said
clapped and slapped towards our table
nice, looking gorgeously sexy, was on
est French kiss ever filmed at the
way after that events seemed to take
and as a result I'm almost ashamed
to say all is forgiven and undying love
can tell you – from the great authority o
Year – is that there's nothing qui
settles on a battlefield after i
and no loving like that of a
Janice these past eight mo
lit fires I never kne
If you can
membership in a wee
corrupt than I cred
Please ri
No 1 River Mews,
disasters strike. I
disguise in case Amand
no women in the pavili
Astonishingly Cli
violinist as a fiddler.

All the best,

Harry.

ATHENS 1100 HRS JUNE 21
CABLE DESPATCH TO: JANICE BLAKEMORE
1 RIVER MEWS LONDON W4 UK EFFING
GREEK POST MANGLED LETTER HARRY
PIERS SUGGESTS YOUVE WON HUGE
CONGRATS STOP WE AWAY SHACK IDIOT
MAID CLAIMED ENGLISH LADY EXCITED
PHONECALLS UNDERSTOOD NOTHING
STOP NOW YOU PERMANENTLY UN-
OBTAINABLE PRESUMABLY CELEBRATING
BEDWARDS HARRY FORTUNATE LOUSE
LETTER FOLLOWING BRAVO CENTRE
COURT BECKONS STOP LOVE RUTH

Dear Venus,

I'm amazed, impressed, in awe, furious – none the less – a triumph *summa cum laude*.

Piers says you phoned confirming the half-message he received from Harry. I wonder which of the embassy wives is at this very minute sweating blood over the other half of the torn letter.

So the count of Nos 1 to 10 is complete, and you've earned your permanent place beneath the royal box at Wimbledon. Not quite as honourably as you might, I may say: seducing your husband is *not* in the Queensbury Rules, even if you did apparently conduct the foreplay on television. However, this is no time to quibble about a foul punch, and you deserve your place in the sun. Which you shall have, though not quite as soon as promised, I'm afraid – we're delayed a couple of days because Piers has gone down with flu. At least so he claims: my view is that he's been scheming all along to be your tenth and is now laid low with disappointment. If terminal impotence sets in I'll know I'm right.

I shall miss our exchanges on the noble art. I feel quite sad. It's been like following the best sit-com ever devised. I've grown fond of your street victims; even though I've never met any of them, I feel I know them all – their public and private faces, their public and private parts. Frankly, I don't believe I would fancy any of them: not enough *chutzpah*, not enough romance. Except Kevin, maybe, and for all his willy-waving he sounds more like a big bad brother than a big bad lover. But then of course I did have Jean-Claude (oh dearly departed). And I do have Piers. He may be balding, he may be boring, he may have piles, he may treat me like an errant child; but he's a man, and the man I love. He's even good in bed when he puts his mind to it, whereas I don't believe I have a mind to put anywhere; just a hatchery for foolish fancies. Perhaps I have a fool's wisdom. Piers says so – he who is neither foolish nor wise, just pragmatically himself, a born ambassador-to-be in spite of the handicap of possessing the least ambassadorial wife in the world.

So there we are. Congratulations to you both. I may even have to learn to endure Harry.

Love as ever, and see you very soon. Row G, Seat 94. It's yours for keeps.

Ruth.

Willirising School
Cerne Abbas
Dorset

Saturday

Dear Mum and Dad

Tried to ring you this morning, then remembered Dad'd be at Lords with Uncle Piers and you Mum would be at Wimbledon like you said with Auntie Ruth. Wot's a debencher seat anyway, and are they comfortable? Does Dad have to ware one of those disgusting ties like all the other wrinklies? Thanks a lot for the present, its great – better than the school one – Im having a bit of trubble with the Pagernini but Mozart's easy-peasy and Liszt's okay if you like that sort of thing. We slortered Wimborne Juniors today – highest score ever at school – afterwards cort Mr Mason undressing the new matron – she's a funny shape. Charley's got pinkeye. Dad, are you going to get a super job now you've got the top prize and decided to live with Mum – why did you? Looking forward to the summer hols

love from

Clive.

September

POSTSCRIPT

2701 Pennsylvania Ave
Washington, DC
USA

September 30th

Dearest Ruth,

The briefest note to say, 'We've arrived.'

Harry started the new job last week, and a new affair this week. So here we go again. Back into training. But – blimey – look at our new address! I may have to regard River Mews as a practice run – easy-peasy, as Clive would say.

Think I'll give the Justice Department a miss, and you'll be glad to hear the French embassy is elsewhere.

But isn't No 1600 the White House?

Ah well!

Love as always,

Janice.

PS This is 'The End' for now. But more later – I promise.